THE MUSTANG MEN

Somewhere in the wilds of Texas, a ruthless outlaw gang discovers that a fortune in gold is just waiting to be taken. However, two lawmen are closing in on the gang. Unknown to all parties, though, a group of riders are risking their necks trying to capture a massive herd of wild horses for the cavalry. Soon it is they who find themselves embroiled in a bloody battle that will change all their lives. These riders are the Mustang Men.

DALE MIKE ROGERS

THE MUSTANG MEN

Complete and Unabridged

LINFORD
Leicester

First published in Great Britain in 2002 by
Robert Hale Limited
London

First Linford Edition
published 2004
by arrangement with
Robert Hale Limited
London

ISBN 1–84395–132–0

Published by
F. A. Thorpe (Publishing)
Anstey, Leicestershire

Set by Words & Graphics Ltd.
Anstey, Leicestershire
Printed and bound in Great Britain by
T. J. International Ltd., Padstow, Cornwall

This book is printed on acid-free paper

Dedicated to my sister,
Christina Margaret

1

It was a hot merciless landscape which faced the solitary rider as he held his pinto mount in check atop a high ridge. A land where sandstone-coloured mountains rose in all directions casting giant shadows across countless canyons below him. This was like no other place the rider had ever been before, not even in his darkest nightmares.

Yet this was the place he had been told would reap him the richest harvest of his entire life. A fortune lay in wait for him to find and claim somewhere down in the canyons. The rider did not seek gold or silver like others of his brand, but something far more lucrative to a man who knew the laws of demand and supply. For here amongst the towering spires of golden rocks, it was said, ran vast herds of the wild mustangs he so desperately sought.

Herds so huge, they beggared belief.

But where were they? From his high perilous perch, he could not see any trace of the horses he knew roamed this alien land in such profusion. He knew that to track them, he had to ride down into the scorching belly of this simmering place. It was an endeavour he did not relish.

To a less knowledgeable soul, this harsh landscape would have meant nothing. But to the rider who rested his wrists on his saddle horn and squinted down at the awesome scenery, this was the place he had been seeking for over a month. It matched the description he had been given exactly.

This was a land designed by the Devil himself and it tested all who ventured into it. There were no borders here to warn the innocent of where they were and what they were about to discover. Nothing to indicate that anyone had ever returned from the belly of this unholy place. Only Satan held any true claim of ownership on what lay silently before him.

If this place had a name at all, it was known only to the circling buzzards who hovered high above the jagged peaks.

He glanced heavenward and wondered if they were waiting for him to die. This country looked more than capable of killing the unwary.

The rider lifted his canteen and slowly unscrewed its stopper as he surveyed every shadow below him. Sipping at the warm water he knew this job was probably going to be the most dangerous of any he had undertaken during his long eventful life. He had seen many things during his two-score years, but nothing had come close to making him feel the way he felt now as he watched the shimmering heat haze rising off the rocks and sand below.

It seemed as though no living creature could possibly survive amid the baking canyons he stared at as water traced down his unshaven features. Yet he knew he was wrong. The Devil himself had designed this place to keep men away. Men who did not have the resolve of this determined soul.

He had to find those horses wherever they were hiding. This might just be his last chance at making his fortune. Life offered few chances for men such as himself. This, he knew, was one of those rare opportunities. He had to grab it before someone else did. There was no alternative.

During his life he had done things most men would never have even contemplated, just to make a dollar. Most of his enterprises had fallen far short of the target he had set himself. Most of the jobs had not earned him enough to pay for one of his gold fillings, yet he continued.

For men such as Tan Gibson never quit whilst there was still breath in their bodies. They were driven by an optimism not found in wealthier men.

Three months earlier, Gibson had gotten wind that the cavalry required mounts for its ever expanding network

4

of forts. Hundreds of mounts, perhaps even thousands. As the army ventured further and further west they found the horses they brought with them totally unsuited for the harsh terrain and climate. They required horses that were used to this uncompromising land. Horses that were totally opposite to the animals raised far away, on the Eastern pastures.

Mustangs!

Gibson knew that the army would not find any ranchers in this country either willing or able to sell off their livestock, whatever the price offered. Out here, the blades of grass were sparse.

If there were ten horses on a ranch, it was because the rancher required exactly ten horses. Not nine nor eleven. With cattle and hogs competing for the meagre shoots of grass that sprouted on the endless ranges that wound their way between the deadly mountains and innumerable canyons, men were accurate with their stock.

Tan Gibson knew the cavalry would find no horses for sale in this hostile climate, but there were horses. Millions of wild horses filling the canyons. Herds that roamed free as they had done ever since the Spanish had released their mounts on to the plains.

It seemed impossible that so few animals could have multiplied into such massive herds in only a couple of centuries. Yet they had. The Indians had quickly learned to capture and tame their spirited hearts, and the tribes who had done it best had in turn become the most successful. Yet the Indians did not require many horses compared to the sheer volume of animals that roamed the untamed West. As the buffalo declined; it seemed as if the horse went from strength to strength. Adapting to each and every climate within a single generation, the mustang herds continued multiplying unhampered.

But though they roamed in numbers beyond even Tan Gibson's wildest imaginings, they were not something one ran into often. For herds went where men seldom ventured. No mountain pass was too high or daunting for the mustangs. It was if they were driven by the memory of what their ancestors had once been and would go anywhere rather than lose their freedom again. Yet once tamed, there was no better horse a rider could find than the mustang.

Gibson knew that a fortune of unshod animals waited for someone such as he, to be brave enough to risk his neck and capture them. Every horse was money in the bank for the lean rider. All he had to do was rope them and then drive them to the nearest cavalry fort.

It sounded easy if you did not give it too much thought.

Sitting tall in his saddle, Gibson stared down from his vantage point at the unfamiliar landscape before him. This place was like another world to the Texan. He had never seen a view less welcoming than this.

It was like staring in through the gates of Hell. A world which was luring him to its bosom. He knew instinctively that this place was deadly.

He could smell it.

Tan Gibson pulled out a long thin cigar and broke it into two equal lengths. One he returned to his jacket breast-pocket, the other he gripped between his teeth. It was too hot to smoke, he thought as he struck a match across his saddle horn and lifted its flame to the tip of the cigar. Gibson sucked on the weed until his lungs were filled with the putrid smoke, then exhaled slowly. Glancing over his broad shoulder, he wondered how long it would take for the rest of his team of wranglers to catch up with him and reach this spot. He had left a trail that a blind man could have followed as he had scouted ahead of his men, but he knew that, unlike himself, they were not in a hurry.

Returning his attention on what lay

before his eyes, Gibson vainly tried to get an inkling of which of the numerous canyons might prove the most likely route to his goal.

It was an impossible task even for one as skilled as he.

Where were the mustangs?

This was where he had been told he would find the largest herd of mustangs anyone had ever set eyes upon. Mustangs who roamed freely through the endless canyons. Looking down into one canyon after another, Gibson wondered if his information was actually correct. There was no sign of the elusive herd or herds. None at all.

But all the same, Gibson knew they were down there somewhere, hiding from the prying eyes of creatures such as himself.

Every sinew in his body told him to be excited whilst his keen mind reminded him of the dangers such animals posed to the foolhardy. Gibson had hunted smaller herds for the last three years further south and had had half the bones in his body broken by the unpredictable creatures. Wild mustangs were an unforgiving bunch. They took no prisoners. A wild horse was the most dangerous creature on God's earth when faced with the loss of the one thing it held precious. Its freedom.

It was said that only a fool or an extremely brave man would willingly risk his neck to hunt down and capture wild horses.

Tan Gibson was no fool.

He was a rare soul.

He was a mustang man.

2

Tan Gibson tied his reins around a heavy rock at the feet of his pinto and then edged closer to the rim of the high sand-rock precipice. The trail down into the maze of canyons veered sharply to his right. It was not the route a novice would or could even contemplate, but to a skilled horseman like Gibson it posed only intrigue. The temptation of simply riding down to the hot floor of the strange rocky configuration was growing with every passing second. Gibson had to wait for the others who were coming to help him on this bold adventure.

He removed his Stetson and wiped the sweat from his brow as his eyes battled against the blinding sun bouncing off the rocks and sand. This was torture to a man of Gibson's spirit, to wait and watch until his team of wranglers finally caught up with the well-marked trail he had left. Yet he was too experienced to deviate from their tried and trusted way of doing things. As their leader, he had to show he could obey his own rules. But it was mighty tempting.

Then Tan Gibson heard something.

It was not a noise he had ever heard before and yet it gave the impression of a rolling thunder storm. Gibson replaced his hat on his head and pulled the brim down to shade his eyes. It sure sounded like thunder, he thought, yet there were no angry clouds in the sky above him.

Suddenly it dawned on him. The sound was coming from below him, down in one of the canyons.

Gibson could feel the hairs on the nape of his neck tingling with anticipation as he crouched down and studied the contrasting areas of brilliant light and blackest of shadows. The shimmering air boiled as he squinted into it.

Could this be the sound of the herd

of elusive mustangs?

Perhaps there were more than one herd and this was just one of them charging unseen from one secret place to another, seeking food and water that only they knew existed. Gibson lifted the ends of his bandanna, wiped his face dry and concentrated on the scene.

The echoing noise of countless hoofs filled his ears and yet he still had no idea of where the galloping horses were. There were just too many canyons. Too many choices.

The sound was bouncing off the highest peaks as he straightened up and reluctantly moved back to the side of his waiting mount. Then he saw the look in the eyes of the nervous pinto. It was the look of an animal who knew exactly what was causing the sound that was filling the ears of both of them. The pinto snorted and strained against the heavy rock which held the reins firmly. Somewhere in the depths of its memory, it knew there were others of its own kind real close; running free.

'Easy, boy,' Gibson said as he ran a calm hand down the long nose of the animal. 'Ain't nothing for you to go fretting about.'

His words soothed the trusting creature, as did the canteen water which the rider had poured into his upturned hat and placed before its forelegs.

As the horse drank, Gibson stared down at the strange landscape once more.

Then he saw it.

For a second, Gibson did not trust that his own eyes were being honest with him, and rubbed them hard with his rough knuckles. Two days' worth of trail dust fell from his eyebrows.

Tan Gibson knew that this was no mirage created by the heat haze. This was real.

It was a plume of dust at least a half-mile long. It could be clearly seen rising from beyond the largest of the walls of golden-coloured rock. By the sheer length of the plume, Gibson could tell that it was being thrown up by a massive herd of running animals.

As this was not cattle country and he knew of no other creatures who herded together in such numbers, Gibson felt certain this dust trail was being kicked up by galloping horses.

No small herd could have created that much dust, Tan Gibson thought. Watching the plume stretch to an incredible length, the mustang hunter began nodding to himself. If there was only one herd down there amongst the countless canyons, it had to be the largest single one ever encountered.

Larger than even he had imagined.

The sound reached almost deafening proportions before he spotted the powerful black stallion far below him. Gibson stepped once more to the very edge of the high ridge as if hypnotized by the beautiful animal. This was the leader of the herd. Gibson could tell by the sheer arrogance of the magnificent animal.

Then through the thick dust-cloud

emerged more horses. Horses of every colour imaginable. There were mares and colts as well as foals and less regal stallions. All of them in hot pursuit of the black stallion.

'Mustangs!' Gibson gasped. There was the sound of disbelief in his voice as he gazed upon the colourful vision. It seemed that this herd was enormous and it appeared to Gibson like a fast flowing river of prime horseflesh.

Briefly Gibson attempted to count them but had given up when his mind calculated that at least two hundred galloping horses had raced from the canyon. Yet that had been at least a whole minute earlier and the herd showed no signs of coming to an end just yet.

They were at least ten abreast and had been racing continuously out of the canyon after the black stallion since it had first emerged.

There appeared to be no end to this wild procession of equine splendour. They just kept on coming from out of the black shadows. Now he felt the noise agonizingly painful as it bounced off the rocks all around him.

It seemed as if all the mountains were starting to shake with the sheer power of the galloping herd.

Even the ground beneath his high-heeled boots was beginning to vibrate as the river of mustangs continued to thunder over the ground beneath his high perch. Gibson was standing totally still and yet he could hear his spurs jangling. The information that had brought him to this place had been correct. This was no normal-sized herd he was staring at wide-eyed.

Thousands! There must be thousands of them! Gibson exclaimed under his breath as he tried to remain calm.

Even when the choking dust obscured the mustangs from view and reached his high vantage point. Tan Gibson was still muttering in disbelief under his breath, the words: Thousands of them!

3

The sight of his crew cautiously edging their wagons and horses up the trail behind him calmed Tan Gibson. It was the only thing that could manage this difficult task. His heart had been beating like a war drum since he had seen the herd of mustangs. Now his eyes focused on the faces of his friends.

There might have been only six of them but they were worth a hundred lesser souls. Gibson struck a match across his brass belt-buckle and cupped its flame in his rough hands. Sucking the smoke into his lungs he sighed heavily. There were enough horses in this hell-hole to keep them busy for months, he thought. Maybe even years.

Grabbing his reins in his left hand, Gibson walked down to greet his men. He knew they would probably think that he was plumb loco when he told them of what he had witnessed less than an hour earlier, but did not care.

He knew it was the truth.

High up on the driver's seat of the first wagon, Gibson noticed the smiling face of the oldest member of his team beaming down at him. The smile was unmistakable and belonged to a silver-haired man named Fred Scott. The smile was also store-bought.

Hauling on the reins of the wagon, Scott brought his four-horse team to a halt beside the tall figure of Gibson.

'Well, I found you.'

'Took ya long enough, Fred,' Gibson said as he tied the reins of his pinto to the wagon's brake-pole and then handed the cigar to the older man seated above him.

'You look plain tuckered, boy,' Scott noted while he puffed on the cigar.

'I am tuckered, damn tuckered.' Gibson turned his head and watched as the second wagon stopped behind the first and the four riders began to dismount beside him.

'This place is hotter than Hell itself, Tan,' Joe Green complained as he opened the lid of one of the wagon water-barrels and scooped out a ladle of the refreshing liquid.

'Too hot to find any mustangs around here, and that's for sure,' added a red-whiskered wrangler known only as Rainbow.

'I've been to hotter places than this, Rainbow,' Keno Smith muttered as he rested his spine against the sunbaked side of the wagon. Smith was the sort who had always been somewhere or done something before anyone else.

'Rainbow's right, Tan. We ain't likely to find any horses in these parts.' Scott sighed heavily as his eyes surveyed the seemingly arid landscape.

Gibson watched the second wagon-driver climb carefully to the ground and then start to rub his britches as if trying to awaken the muscles in his legs.

'You OK, Rufas?' he asked.

Rufas Blake looked up with the saddest eyes any of the wranglers had ever encountered. His was a soul burdened by life itself.

'I've been better, Tan.'

'Still got the aches?' Gibson enquired, trying not to allow his smile to be seen by the morbid-faced man.

'I reckon I got the rheumatism, Tan,' Blake replied as he inspected his joints.

'I thought you had swamp fever, Rufas?' Sol Dane grinned from behind his youthful yellow whiskers whilst tethering his mount to the spokes of the first wagon.

'That was last week, Sol,' Rainbow laughed loudly.

'You might mock but I'm a sick man,' Blake said as he slowly walked towards the other men.

'But you're still as strong as an ox, Rufas,' Tan Gibson added when the man reached the dust-caked group of wranglers.

Rufas Blake almost smiled when he heard the flattering words aimed in his direction.

'That was before I had me the swamp

fever. Now I'm as weak as a kitten.'

'So weak and feeble that you can handle a four-horse team for eight straight hours?' Gibson raised an eyebrow.

'That just takes a little practice, Tan.' Blake shrugged as he felt the colour rising in his cheeks.

There were still a few hours of daylight remaining but Gibson had no desire to do anything this day. He wanted to sleep and dream of the thousands of wild horses he had seen with his own eyes. He wanted to have at least eight hours to rest his weary bones for what he knew lay ahead.

Gibson had no reason to ruin his chances with what he knew lived in the mysterious canyons. This was too big a deal for him or his team of wranglers to get wrong. There was far too much at stake.

If they only managed to capture half the mustangs he had seen and heard, they would all be wealthy men. This was no job for the amateur.

There was only one way to do this.

It had to be done right.

It had to be done his way.

To all appearances they were a motley-looking bunch, but looks can often be misleading. This was one of those cases. Each of them had been hand-picked by Tan Gibson himself back in Dodge City.

They were all the best mustang men he knew. Some almost as good as him. There were no hangers-on in this well-oiled team of wranglers. He had worked with each of them and knew them inside out. Capturing wild horses was dangerous and Tan Gibson only surrounded himself with men he could rely upon. Each would risk his own life for any of the others without a second thought for his own safety.

In a profession of such deadly uncertainty, there was no room for men whom you could not trust. Trust had to be there at all times between the members of the team. Never spoken of or given a second thought. An unwritten rule which glued them all together.

Tan Gibson was smiling at his men.

'That's a heck of a big smile, Tan,' Fred Scott observed, tossing the butt of his smoke away.

'I got me a good reason to be showing these teeth,' Gibson explained as he squared up to his half-dozen followers.

'You found them?' Joe Green asked with a trembling tone in his voice. A tone which teetered on the edge of disbelief.

'Yep! I found the beauties, boys!'

'How many horses you seen, Tan? How many?' Sol Dane asked excitedly.

'Hard to figure exactly.' Gibson found his tongue tracing across his dry lips as the memory of the massive herd of mustangs filled his thoughts once again.

'Hundreds?'

'Nope.'

'Thousands?'

'Yep!'

'Are you serious, Tan?' Rainbow edged close enough to the taller man and studied the weathered features. 'Thousands of mustangs out here in this dust-bowl?'

'I'm damn serious, Rainbow. I seen me the biggest darn herd of wild mustangs anybody ever set eyes upon.' Tan Gibson kicked at the dry dusty ground before finally succumbing to the sheer joy which swelled his chest to bursting point. 'And they're all ours!'

The yell echoed off the sand rock all about them. Before it had ceased, it was joined by the cheers of the six other mustang men.

4

The sun was low and the sky a crimson blaze as sunset rapidly approached. The shadows which trailed from the line of riders across the sandy ground were black like the hearts of the mounted men themselves. Night was coming quickly now, but these riders continued on their chosen course as if unaware of anything except the reason which had brought them to this dry inhospitable place.

If anywhere resembled Hell itself, it was here. The Devil would have been right at home in this torturous place. Perhaps that was why the riders seemed totally oblivious to the heat and just kept on riding.

They numbered an even dozen. Each little better than the other and twice as dangerous as most normal men. For these were anything but normal men who sat astride the line of lathered-up horses as they continued on towards their ultimate goal. This was one of the most deadly bunches of riders ever to gather together anywhere.

For this was the notorious Brody gang. Or what was left of it. Once there had been five Brody brothers with a score of followers. Now only Cole Brody remained in the land of the living at the head of the meanest bunch of infamous killers. Still able to control what remained of his gang by the sheer strength of his character and skill with his matched pair of Remington .45s, Cole Brody rode like the man he was: arrogantly. Now in his sixtieth year he had buried all his younger siblings one by one as their luck had slowly started to run out. He knew there were few years left for a man such as himself to continue in this profession and he required one big paying job, if he were ever to retire alive.

This was why he was leading his men towards their distant objective. Cole

Brody knew that one way or another, this would be his final chance.

The line of horsemen had been riding for eight days across the sun-bleached prairie with only one thought filling their combined minds; the fat bank waiting for them in the sleepy town of Pueblo Flats.

There were many gangs of outlaws equally ruthless as this group of riders roaming the West, but none of those had ever dared to strike such a remote spot as the one Pueblo Flats occupied. The sheer terrain that surrounded the remote town was enough to deter most outlaws from even attempting to locate it, let alone rob its solitary bank.

Yet these riders dared.

The Brody gang dared because Cole Brody had decreed it so.

Set on the very edge of the deadly prairie which led to the strange multitude of canyons and towering rock towers, Pueblo Flats existed mainly due to the stubbornness of its hundred or so inhabitants. Wealth had set these souls apart from other less fortunate settlers and settlements that had grown up along the perilous prairie. All the other towns had found the unyielding climate too deadly and had long been deserted and left to the brutal elements to reclaim.

But not Pueblo Flats. It remained and prospered alone in a hundred square miles of arid landscape like a desert oasis. Gold-dust was taken from the fat, swollen vault of the bank regularly to distant towns and exchanged for hard cash. Cash which was used to buy everything required by its citizens.

Secrecy had always been the one thing the people of Pueblo Flats had cherished. For with secrecy they were able to keep their gold to themselves. Year after year, decade after decade, the gold had accumulated until even they had no idea of how much gold there was in their mutually owned bank.

The twelve riders who were now a mere day's ride away from the town knew its secret. They knew how and why it had not only survived but actually continued to prosper.

These riders knew about the narrow river which wound its way through the small township. They also knew about the gold-dust that never failed to fill the pans of Pueblo Flats' citizens whenever they visited the unassuming river.

This knowledge alone kept the dozen members of the Brody gang spurring their lathered-up mounts on and on in defiance of all the hardships this journey pitted against them. Nothing could stop them from reaching Pueblo Flats now. Now they could almost smell the gold in their nostrils, luring them like bears to a beehive.

Pueblo Flats had survived against all odds with its secret intact for thirty years and had prevented a goldrush from destroying their fragile community, but although their secret had been guarded for over three decades, it had taken a mere matter of minutes to destroy.

That had been eight days earlier in a saloon in a town called Ravens Creek.

It had only taken the words of one drunken man from Pueblo Flats to find the ears of the leader of the dozen riders. Words which made the listener realize that unlike his five dead brothers, he might just be able to die rich.

Thirty years of well-guarded secrecy had been wiped out in a mere blink of a bloodshot eye.

Cole Brody had placed a well-aimed bullet into that bloodshot eye after he had learned all there was to learn about Pueblo Flats.

5

Ravens Creek was a sprawling town which covered at least sixty acres of land covered in dusty soil and yellow grass. No wild animals would have been loco enough to live here but men seemed to find it totally suitable for their needs. For unlike the noble creatures of the wilderness, men sought and found different things to give them pleasure. Ravens Creek had survived because it provided even the most depraved of souls with what they wanted. Brothels brought in trade from a hundred miles radius and never failed to deliver what the customers required for their hard-earned cash. It was also the home of fifty gambling halls and saloons and had boasted of having not only a sheriff but four full-time deputies.

But as with all boasts, it had proved

ironic. Five law officers who were more used to taking their cut of all the immoral earnings were no match for real gunfighters. Theirs was an illusion which had never been tested. For that had been before the notorious Cole Brody and his gang had visited the sprawling town. Before the sheriff and his men had made their biggest and final mistake.

Ravens Creek no longer had law officers but an unexpectedly prosperous undertaker who had seen his profits soar, as it was left to him to bury the bodies which had been left in the wake of the Brody gang's ruthless rampage.

Darkness fell over Ravens Creek as it had done every night since the dozen heavily armed outlaws had ridden away from the bloody carnage they had created.

Yet this night was to be unlike those previous ones. For on this night, the law would return to the boisterous town, even if only for the briefest of spells.

Mayor Thadius McBride had been a

broken man since witnessing the entire Ravens Creek law force being cut down a mere week earlier. His was a mind unable to grasp how deadly real gunfighters could be. How it was all his fault for sending tax collectors with tin stars pinned to their shirts and vests to try and arrest one who, he had assumed, was merely a fat elderly gunman.

After Cole Brody had shot dead the drunken man from distant Pueblo Flats, it had been McBride who had insisted his sheriff and all the town's deputies should go and arrest the killer. If any man had made a greater error of judgement, the mayor did not know of any, apart from the sheriff who had blindly done as he was instructed.

Obeying Mayor McBride's instructions, the shotgun-toting lawmen had entered the saloon in force and made their way to where Cole Brody was drinking beside the lifeless body. Wiser men might have sensed the danger even then, but not Ravens Creek's lawmen.

Being a man of bombastic self-importance, the mayor had followed the officers into the saloon urging them to dispatch their duties and arrest the offender. What then took place was carved deeply into his memory for all time.

It had been a bloodbath.

McBride could still see the image of Cole Brody as he sat passively at the round card-table, glass in one hand and a bottle of rye in the other. The man had looked unlike any killer he had ever imagined in his wildest nightmares.

The stout figure aged at least sixty had not even blinked as the sheriff and deputies had approached him. It was as if he either did not care or was simply totally unafraid. Either way, he did not look the sort of man who lived by the gun. Again, looks can often be misleading.

In this case, they were totally misleading.

Perhaps it was because Cole Brody had not tried to exchange either his bottle or his glass for a pistol which had lured the lawmen into his trap. It might have just been the fact that Brody simply looked nothing more than a plump old drifter as he sat drinking.

McBride stepped out on to the porch of the now empty sheriff's office and stared out at the dark streets as he recalled the horrific scene within that saloon, once again.

As the sheriff and his men had reached the card-table where Brody sat and waved their shotguns at the dispassionate outlaw leader, the mayor remembered how the men leaning against the long bar had suddenly turned with their arsenal of cocked weaponry in their hands and aimed them at the law officers.

Not a single word had been uttered by any of the dozen or so strangers as they emptied their guns and rifles into the bodies of the hapless deputies and sheriff. McBride had stood at the swing-doors of the saloon and watched as the entire law enforcement of Ravens

Creek was ripped to shreds by countless rounds of ammunition. None of the
outlaws stopped firing until their
weapons were empty and Cole Brody
remained seated during the entire sixty
seconds of mayhem. The outlaw leader
just continued swallowing his rye and
refilling his glass until the room was
awash with blood and gore.

Only when it was over, did the stout
figure stand and raise a glass at his
men.

McBride was still haunted by the
smile across the puffy face of the man
who he was to learn later, was Cole
Brody. A face which was branded into
his brain for ever.

The mayor stepped across the board-
walk, struck a match and lit the solitary
lantern hanging on the wooden wall.
Then he tossed the match away and
leaned heavily on a porch upright. If
sleep were meant to help ease a
tortured mind such as his, he longed for
the moment when he could actually
close his eyes and find more than a few

fleeting minutes of it. Yet the dreams came quickly each night and woke him up soaked in his own sweat.

McBride stared inside the empty office and wondered if he would ever be able to find anyone willing to take on the jobs of sheriff and deputies again.

He had tried to hire replacement lawmen, but it seemed as if there was not a single soul within the boundaries of Ravens Creek who wanted a job where death could come so swiftly.

Thadius McBride listened to the loud reckless sounds which were filling the streets of Ravens Creek. It was the sound of people freed from the restrictions men wearing tin stars were paid to keep in check. Fifty saloons and gambling halls were now doing what they did best with the knowledge that, at least for the time being, there was no one to stop them, no outstretched hands waiting to be paid off to turn a blind eye.

As he searched vainly for his pipe in his deep pockets, McBride saw something at the edge of the long street. It was a pair of riders illuminated by the moon and street-lanterns. For a brief moment, the mayor felt his heart pounding inside his undershirt. Then as the riders drew closer he began to calm down as his eyes focused on the gleaming stars pinned to their top coats.

The horsemen allowed their mounts to walk slowly up to the hitching rail outside the sheriff's office before reining in.

'My name's Marshal Vincent and this is my deputy, Ericson.'

McBride moved closer to the two men seated astride their tall horses. He had neither seen nor heard or them before but could not hide his gratitude that at least the law had returned to Ravens Creek once more.

'Welcome, Marshal Vincent. I'm Thadius McBride, the town mayor. Thank God you've come.'

'I heard tell you had yourself a little trouble here a week back, McBride.'

'You heard of the slaughter?'

'We heard,' Ericson answered from behind his black beard.

'But how?'

'News travels fast, McBride,' Vincent said as his eyes flashed in the light of the porch lantern. 'You got any idea who these varmints were?'

'It was Cole Brody and his gang, Marshal.'

The two riders dismounted slowly and looped their reins over the hitching pole before stepping up on to the boardwalk next to the sweating mayor. They seemed to pause for a while as the sound of the saloons reached their ears. Then they walked into the sheriff's office and studied it with interest.

'Cole Brody?' Vincent repeated the name as he rested a boot on top of one of the hard-back chairs and started removing his spurs.

'Yes, Marshal. It was Cole Brody and he had at least a dozen men with him,' McBride gushed excitedly.

Vincent's eyes flashed across at Ericson.

'Looks like we have found the scent again, *amigo*.'

'Yeah, for a while there I thought the old fox had managed to give us the slip,' Ericson replied as he checked the empty coffee-pot on top of the unlit stove.

McBride stepped up to the tall marshal.

'You know of Brody?'

'We sure do, partner,' Vincent drawled.

'He's the reason we're here,' Ericson added.

6

As dawn broke across the strange landscape of towering sand-coloured spires and slowly traced over the spiders-web of canyons, the five riders carefully descended atop their cutting horses as the two wagons cautiously followed. The trail was only just wide enough for the large-wheeled vehicles to negotiate whilst their skilled drivers held the snorting six-horse teams in check.

This was no place for either the moronic Rufas Blake or the feisty Fred Scott to relax their iron grips on the heavy leather reins or reduce the pressure on the brake-poles beneath their boots. As the morning sky began to glow above their heads, both drivers used every muscle in their legs and arms simply in order to maintain their total control of the nervous teams of horses in their charge.

Sweat poured down the faces of both wagon drivers. It was the sweat of total concentration.

There was barely eighteen inches to spare to either side of the prairie schooners as they slowly followed Tan Gibson and his wranglers down to the floor of the canyon. Yet, for both the drivers, this was merely another chance to display not only their expertise but their bravery.

Tan Gibson had allowed his pinto to find its own way down the dry trail whilst keeping both eyes fixed on the wagons behind him. For although he knew that there were no men more capable of handling six-horse teams anywhere, he worried. No matter how good a wagon driver might be, it only took one of those six horses to spook for it all to go fatally wrong.

To some it might have seemed foolhardy even to contemplate bringing the heavy vehicles down such a dangerous incline, but Gibson knew that once they were on the flat canyon floor, he could make good use of them.

Somewhere within the twisting gulches and canyons of this unholy place, there were thousands of wild horses. Stampeding cattle were bad enough but they could not hold a candle to mustangs on the hoof. The sheer size of the wagons could be used as barricades if necessary. They also provided much needed protection for his men.

Mustangs feared little when charging wildly from one point to another but were ten times as dangerous and unpredictable when confined to places such as this. Should the beautiful black stallion lead his massive herd of galloping mustangs unexpectedly out of any of the mouths of the numerous canyons, Tan Gibson knew the animals would not willingly come anywhere near his covered wagons.

For even wild horses would never willingly step on something if it could be avoided and they would certainly never come anywhere near objects as alien as canvas-topped wagons, if there was an alternative.

Apart from that, mustangs were completely unpredictable.

Placed near a wall of natural rock, with enough space for their cutting horses and wagon-teams to be safely corralled, Tan Gibson knew he and his men would be safe beneath the flat beds of the pair of prairie schooners during the dark nights they would have to spend in this place. The wagons were his only life insurance. Without them, it would be impossible to remain.

The air was cool and crisp as Tan Gibson watched Fred Scott skilfully driving his well-equipped vehicle on to the level ground with Rufas Blake's wagon in close pursuit. He gave a huge sigh of relief and wiped his brow with his shirt-sleeve.

'That was a close 'un, Tan,' Rainbow said. He held his reins firmly to his chest as he came alongside the pinto rider.

'Yep. Them boys didn't have a lot of spare sand to work with on that trail,' Gibson agreed as he chewed on the butt of his cigar.

'How we gonna get them wagons back out of here?'

Gibson eyed Rainbow.

'We've plenty of time to figure that one out.'

The five riders spurred their mounts and followed the pair of rocking wagons for several hundred yards along the dry dusty ground.

Gibson urged his pinto to catch up with the first wagon and raised his arm to Scott. The older man forced his right leg down on the brake-pole and hauled back on his reins.

The wagon stopped.

'We stopping here, boy?' Scott raised a white eyebrow as the question left his lips. 'It's kinda dry here and my team need water. A lot of water. More water than we got left in them water-barrels.'

Gibson stood in his stirrups as his

fellow horsemen gathered around his pinto.

'I know that, Fred. The thing is, I ain't got no idea where the nearest water-hole is.'

Scott stared up at the ragged peaks and the sun, which was now casting its warmth against them. A warmth which would soon become heat. Deadly unforgiving heat. A heat which could burn the hide off a man in hours if he paid it no mind.

'I don't cotton to this place, Tan. It's no place for living men like us. This place is where bones get bleached.'

'There has to be water in this hell-hole, Fred. That herd of mustangs couldn't survive without there being an awful lot of water around here some-place,' Gibson drawled. 'Water and grass.'

'But where in tarnation is this water and grass, Tan?' Scott asked rubbing the palms of his blistered hands anxiously down his shirt-front.

'All I gotta do is find it.' Gibson

smiled as he returned his seat to the saddle and turned the pinto full circle to face his wranglers. 'Rainbow comes with me to scout out some of these canyons.'

'What'll we do, Tan?' Sol Dane chirped anxiously as he held his horse in check.

'You boys can make camp and water the horses from the water-barrels, Sol,' Gibson said firmly.

'But how on earth can you find a water-hole with so many canyons to choose from? It'll take a month of Sundays.' Joe Green rubbed his chin thoughtfully.

'Even unshod horses leave tracks, Joe.' Gibson nodded to Rainbow and the two riders rode away from the group.

Each of the watching mustang men knew that if anyone could locate a supply of fresh water, it was their leader. He was a man who never quit anything once he started. They watched as Gibson and Rainbow cantered along the dry ground until they disappeared into the black shadows. It was only early but already they could feel the temperature rising all about them. Fred Scott was right; this was no place for living men.

7

The inhabitants of Pueblo Flats were not usually the sort to greet the dawn. They had no call even to try. With money and gold enough to ignore the roosters which greeted each new day, they had managed to keep their secret wealth from the rest of the outside world for three decades.

Yet as the blazing sun crept slowly into the cloudless blue sky, three men stood shoulder to shoulder silently watching the distant trail across the flat arid landscape. These were not men who chose to be awake but troubled souls who vainly waited for one of their own to return.

They saw nothing.

That was what concerned them.

For the first time in all the years they had been sending members of their small community to distant towns such as Ravens Creek to change their gold-dust into hard cash, the messenger had failed to return.

Each of the menfolk of Pueblo Flats had taken it in turns over the last thirty years to take small bags of gold dust to various assayers' offices in distant towns. Never enough to alert the curious and never the same town twice in succession. That would have aroused suspicion. For all these long years the people of Pueblo Flats had successfully managed to keep their secret from being discovered.

Nothing had ever gone wrong before.

But the three men who watched the sun-bleached trail knew that something must have happened this time. Their messenger should have returned three days earlier, but had not.

Even souls of little imagination within Pueblo Flats had been awake during the previous days and nights, finding sleep an elusive bedfellow. There could be a dozen reasons why he had not returned on time. Each as plausible as the next but only one reason burned in the fretting minds of the three silent men.

He had to be dead. There was no other reasonable explanation.

They had not given the messenger enough gold dust for him to have abandoned his fellow townspeople. Just enough to keep Pueblo Flats' communal prosperity at the level they required to buy anything the town needed.

He might not be dead. Maybe he had gone on a drunken binge with the cash he had gotten for their gold dust, each of the men surmised. If he had managed to get himself into trouble, had he revealed their secret to anyone?

Each of the three men who had not slept for days felt an unease tearing at their innards. They knew the truth was they had sent one of their least capable residents—this time. A man who had a weakness for sour-mash whiskey and long-legged females. A man who had come close to betraying them before.

The men who stood like dust-caked statues on the very edge of Pueblo Flats began to wonder how long their small community might have before they would find out if their worst fears were in fact founded in reality.

Either way, the trio of town elders, Judge Bevis Hogan, Marvin Caine and Arthur Bearcutt, felt they had good reason to be troubled.

There was an overwhelming air of impending doom out on the hot trail as the heat haze silently rose from the cracked ground.

As they turned and made their way back towards the saloon which was filled with free liquor, Hogan broke the silence.

'We ought never to have sent Davies, boys.'

'It was his turn, Judge,' Bearcutt muttered.

'I should have gone instead,' Caine sighed wearily.

The three men mounted the board-walk, pushed open the doors of the saloon, and entered. It was too early to drink but that was exactly what they were going to do. Drink and wait.

8

They had been riding for more than an hour through the dry endless canyon. It seemed far longer to the pair of wranglers as they wiped the sweat from their faces. Gibson had been following the churned-up tracks left by the countless hoofs of the wild mustangs he had witnessed the previous day. Yet the further away from their makeshift camp Gibson and Rainbow got, the more nervous they became.

This was unlike any place either rider had ever found himself in before. It bore no resemblance to anywhere they knew of. The closest thing they could imagine to this was Hell itself. The humidity and heat were beyond anything they had ever experienced in their wildest nightmares. Every stitch of their clothing was soaked by their own ceaseless sweat.

The walls of the massive sand-coloured rocks were now less than twenty feet apart and both riders were silently wondering what would happen should they meet the the same herd of wild horses coming back in the opposite direction.

There was no cover here. Nowhere to hide or take shelter in this narrowing canyon which was fast resembling a tunnel. The shadows were darker the further the pair rode into the unknown and yet the heat was no less merciless.

'I'm starting to get a mite troubled, Tan,' Rainbow said as he drew his horse closer to the walking pinto.

'You and me both, Rainbow,' Gibson retorted. He lifted his canteen to his lips and swallowed the last mouthful of water.

'This ain't no natural place.'

Gibson pointed at the ground before them. 'Them tracks are natural enough. We have to keep tracking them critters until we find us some water.'

'What if that darn herd comes back

this way?' There was genuine concern in the voice of the wrangler.

'If they do, we'll hear them coming long before they reach us. We got plenty of time to turn around and hightail it out of here.' Tan Gibson knew he was correct but found little comfort in his own words.

'Reckon you're right. Reckon we could outrun them mustangs, sure enough.' Rainbow's voice did not sound as though he actually believed what he was saying.

'Quit fretting.'

'I'm sure trying, Tan.' Rainbow forced a grin. 'It ain't easy though.'

Gibson nodded as he hung the empty canteen over his saddle horn and gripped his reins again. For countless mile after mile the pair of mustang men had not seen any sign of there being water in this desolate place. It was as if this entire land of canyons was totally dead. Not even a blade of grass in the shadows to encourage them on. Yet they had to keep following the tracks of the herd.

Gibson and Rainbow had not heard anything except the echoes of their own horses' hoofs since leaving the two wagons and the rest of their team. Not a single noise had reached their ears.

It was as if they, too, like this lifeless place, were dead.

★   ★   ★

Cole Brody knew more than he ever displayed on his smooth round face. He knew the secret of staying alive when all around him found death. He had never felt even the slightest morsel of remorse for all the killings he had perpetrated, ordered or planned. His had been a charmed existence compared to the rest of his brothers. In his six decades of life he had never even been wounded whilst all around him much slimmer men had fallen victim to their enemies' bullets.

Cole Brody knew many things all right.

He knew how to steal. He knew how

to slide a knife silently into anyone who he had decided deserved to die. His was a knowledge few would wish to learn. Yet he was still alive and still the leader of what remained of the infamous Brody gang.

As the twelve riders drove on into yet another new day, he was still at the head of his men, holding reins in one hand as the other rested upon the handle of one of his pistols. For even riding amongst men he had known and led for half his long torrid life, he still waited for the bullet in his back. A bullet which he knew would one day come from one of his own, if the law did not get him first.

Cole Brody rode like a man half his weight.

It was as if his horse feared its master and somehow managed to cope with the stout figure in the saddle. Brody knew he was living on borrowed time. No man of his age or size could possibly avoid the bullets of an enemy for ever. Not even he.

As he gritted his teeth and aimed the horse straight ahead he began to sense signs that they were getting closer to their chosen goal. The scent of smoke filled his keen nostrils. Smoke which he knew came from the chimneys of townspeople.

There was only one town out here in this godforsaken place and that was Pueblo Flats.

Brody did not like this country. It was too hot in the day and yet could freeze a man to death during the night. This was no normal land, but a place where his sort often found themselves forced eventually if they survived long enough.

The twelve horses began to ease up as their leader slowly allowed his mount to stop. Dust swirled about them on the hot air as Brody slowly dismounted.

Without speaking, Cole Brody began to remove his saddle. It was his way to ride through the night and rest up for a couple of hours after the morning sun climbed into the sky. None of his followers knew why, but that had been the way he had always led them. Without even pausing for thought, the ruthless outlaws all began to copy their leader's actions.

It was a strange spot Brody had chosen this time to make camp in. To their right the land rolled away steeply to a place where jagged rocks touched the sky whilst directly ahead the land seemed virtually flat. The morning heat was rising faster than any of them liked and already blurring their view of what lay ahead and what lay behind them. Only the golden rock-spires to their right remained clearly visible.

Brody said nothing as he struck a match and lit a long fat cigar gripped between his teeth and inhaled the strong smoke deep into his lungs. His men knew their duties and did them without his having to say a word. Some tended to the horses. Some the camp-fire whilst others prepared to make coffee and food. They were like a well-oiled machine.

Perhaps that was what they truly were, after so many years together. Nothing more than a mindless machine. No good as individuals but a deadly force when together. It was true they had all learned to do as Cole Brody instructed them without ever questioning him. Others had failed to listen to the words of the stout man and they had died along the way. Even Brody's own brothers had paid the ultimate price for ignoring the instinctive wisdom of their eldest sibling. Those who remained of the gang now seemed either incapable or unwilling to harbour thoughts of their own for fear of what might happen.

Cole Brody sucked on the cigar and wallowed in its flavour as he stepped away from their tethered horses and surveyed the scenery with aged eyes. He could still see well enough when it came to shooting it out in a twenty-foot saloon or bank foyer but distance was now becoming less easy for him to see with any certainty.

But his nose still had all its power.

He could still smell the sweat on a man who feared him. Still catch the aroma of a female when she was in season or simply pleased to see a customer who always paid cash. His nostrils were still able to detect even the faintest hint of a town on the slightest of breezes.

After watering the dozen mounts, a lean figure ambled across the dry dusty ground until he was standing next to the famed Cole Brody. He towered over the solid Brody, yet like all the members of the gang seemed almost subservient to the smaller man.

'You tended the horses, Jones?' Brody's eyes flashed up at the lean man.

'Yep. I tended them good.'

'Rub them down. They're lathered-up bad.'

'I'll rub them down shortly, Cole.'

Cole Brody cast another fleeting stare at the tall Jones.

'What's eating you?'

'I was just wondering what you thinking about, Cole?' Jones asked nervously.

'Pueblo Flats is about twenty miles up wind, Jones,' Brody replied, pointing his cigar at the heat haze.

'How you know that?'

'I can smell it.'

'Smell what?' Jones scratched his head.

'I can smell their fires. Their trash and their women.' Cole Brody grinned as he replaced the cigar between his teeth. It was the smile of a man who meant every word that trailed from his lips.

Jones sniffed at the air but could only smell the acrid aroma of the dry tobacco burning in his leader's mouth.

'You can smell all that?'

'Yep. All of that, and more, Jones.'

'Then how come we don't just carry on?' Jones knew that if they were that close, they could have just continued on until they reached the small town.

Cole Brody blew out a huge cloud of

smoke and shook his head thoughtfully.

'First we gets us some rest. Then we has us some good coffee and vittles in our guts and then when we are all fresh, we ride on for Pueblo Flats.'

'But if Pueblo Flats is twenty miles away, it'll be dark before we gets there, Cole,' Jones said.

'Exactly!'

9

It was a chilling, unnerving sound that both riders had never heard the like of before. Its sheer intensity bore no resemblance to anything the pair of mustang men had ever experienced in their long eventful lives. There was a violence within the volume of chaos that cascaded off the canyon walls all around the two riders. It even frightened their mounts.

Tan Gibson dragged his reins to his chin first and halted his skittish pinto. The mustang hunter called Rainbow reached forward and grabbed the bridle of his mount as he too heard the chilling noise echoing off the vertiginous walls of the narrow canyon. Both riders sat silently in their saddles as the sound grew louder and louder.

The ground beneath the hoofs of their horses began to tremble as the two horsemen fought with every ounce of their strength to keep their mounts in check.

What had at first appeared to be nothing more than a distant thunderstorm, was now beginning to shake every bone in their bodies. This was deadly serious. This was their worst fears becoming reality. Dust began to filter down from the towering sides of the sand-coloured rock formations that flanked them on both sides. Then small stones started to fall all around them as the vibrations became more and more intense.

'Feels like an earthquake, Tan,' Rainbow shouted above the ear-splitting din.

Gibson steered his horse closer to the sweating Rainbow and shouted:

'This ain't no damn earthquake. It's the herd. They're coming back! We gotta get out of here fast, Rainbow.'

Without even bothering to reply, Rainbow turned his horse and jabbed his spurs deep into its flesh. The startled creature raised its head and tried to respond to its master's urgency but failed.

Before Tan Gibson had managed to haul his pinto around to follow his companion, he heard the pitifully agonizing sound of a horse as it hit the ground. Gibson leaned hard to his left and swung his animal about.

As the deafening sound grew louder in the sweltering canyon, Gibson saw his friend lying beside the winded animal. For a moment neither man nor beast seemed able to move.

'Get up, Rainbow!' Gibson yelled at his fallen comrade as he tried desperately to hold his terrified pinto in check.

Somehow the stunned mustang man managed to get to his feet. He hovered beside his stricken horse for a few seconds. Seconds which seemed endless in the minds of both nervous men.

Rainbow vainly tried to get his winded horse to its feet as everything around them began to shake with raw violence. A cloud of dust slowly began to envelop the canyon behind Gibson's skittish mount as he reached down. It was no normal dust-cloud, but a living, breathing cloud of galloping animals.

'Get on up behind me, Rainbow.'

'I can't leave my horse, Tan.'

Gibson wrapped his reins around his left wrist as he offered his right hand again. The sound behind them was now obliterating their words from one another but they knew exactly what the other was saying. Every word was etched in their dust-caked faces.

Rainbow cast a glance backward at the oncoming dust-cloud and saw the images of the wild mustangs bearing down upon them. It was not a sight he would forget in a hurry.

After hesitating for what seemed a lifetime, he accepted the arm of his companion and threw himself up behind Tan Gibson's saddle cantle. The pinto did not require the sting of its master's spurs in order to take flight from the approaching herd which bore down on them in the narrow canyon. It was all Tan Gibson could do to hold on to the reins of his mount as it galloped along the dry trail.

With each stride that the gallant pinto managed to take the pursuers came closer. The wild mustangs were following their black stallion leader and closing the distance between themselves and the fleeing pinto with every heartbeat.

On and on, Gibson urged his mount, but it did not have the power to put any distance between itself and the wild fury which followed.

The herd did not have the burden of two men as well as a saddle and all its livery, upon their backs. They were free of all man-made objects, unlike the pinto. The herd of mustangs was gaining fast.

Rainbow gripped the waist of his friend tightly and stared with terrified eyes over his shoulder at the snorting black stallion as it drew closer and closer to them. Gibson stood high in his stirrups and tried to lean as far forward as possible in an attempt to take weight off the back of his valiant mount. Yet he could tell by the sound of the echoing hoofs that the herd was gaining ground on them.

For endless miles, he and Rainbow had ridden deeper and deeper into this endless canyon as they followed the tracks left by the herd. Sweat-soaked miles along which they had seen the canyon walls draw closer and closer to them until they could have almost touched both sides of the canyon at once. Yet they had continued trailing the tracks of the elusive herd. Tracks which they had known would lead them to water.

Water and deadly danger.

Thirst had forced them relentlessly on when logic had told them they were flirting with death itself in this narrow canyon. What had started out as a search for wild horses had become more a desperate attempt to locate water over the past hours as they had drained their canteens dry.

Now Tan Gibson knew he was faced with an uncertain future which might be only a few fleeting minutes long. His horse was spent and he knew it.

The herd of wild angry creatures was getting terrifyingly closer. Then the mustangs' snorting nostrils seemed to be bearing down upon the two men astride the flagging overburdened pinto. Rainbow's hands gripped the waist of Gibson tighter as the heads of the wild horses began to draw level with their staggering mount.

Feeling Rainbow's tapping fingers on his shoulder, Gibson turned his head and stared at the charging horses which were now all around them.

He knew they could not outrun this herd. The valiant pinto simply did not have the power in its legs beneath them. The mustangs were fresh and filled with the water they had been seeking.

This was a race Gibson knew he could not win.

As the black stallion galloped ahead of his mount, Gibson suddenly realized his folly. He was trying to outrun something which he could not outrun. As more and more of the massive herd thundered past him, he began to pull back on his reins and slow his mount.

These horses were wild and dangerous but appeared totally unaware of the riders upon the back of the exhausted pinto. To these wild beasts, they were not a threat, but simply an obstacle to pass.

Slowly stopping the pinto in the centre of the narrow canyon, both men held on tightly to each other, the saddle and the horse beneath them for dear life. It was a risky thing to do but so was the alternative of continuing to force the pinto into trying to continue running when its legs had no more strength left in them. As long as they could remain astride their trusty mount, Gibson and Rainbow knew that they could not be trampled to death by the wild-eyed herd.

Dozens of galloping mustangs thundered past the motionless pinto every second as the two men prayed that their mount still had enough strength left to remain upright and not be knocked over by the wild horses.

For more than five minutes the herd continued to stream past them as if drawn by a magnet to the hoofs of the black stallion who led them.

Gibson could not see anything as they were totally enveloped in the choking dust-cloud, but knew he dared not relax his firm grip on the pinto for even a second. For to do so, would be to risk being thrown off the back of the tall mount under the merciless unshod hoofs of the galloping mustangs.

Then the two men felt the last of the wild creatures passing them and the deafening sound began to die away slowly into the distance.

'Is that the last of them?' Rainbow asked nervously.

'Reckon so, Rainbow,' Gibson replied as he raised the tails of his bandanna and rubbed the thick dust from his eyes. Slowly he began to regain his sight as the dust fell from his stinging eyes. 'Leastways, I sure hope so.'

Rainbow relaxed his hands and released Gibson from his vice-like grip.

'Thank God. I ain't never been so scared in all my days.'

Tan Gibson tried to spit but there was no spit in his dry mouth. Only dust. Dry choking dust.

'We better head back to where we last seen your horse, Rainbow.'

Rainbow shook his head until he was able to see again. Then he slowly allowed himself to slide off the back of the pinto. For a few moments the noise of the thousands of horses still bounced off the canyon walls. It was a chilling reminder of what they were facing in this devilish place. Gibson's only consolation was that the herd was at least heading away from them now.

Tan Gibson dismounted.

'We have to retrace our tracks back to your mount and then go further on into the canyon, Rainbow.'

Rainbow nodded.

'The water must be close. Them mustangs couldn't have been galloping at that pace for long.'

'I sure hope the boys have everything tied down back at the camp. Otherwise them mustangs will rip right through them.' Tan Gibson looked grim as the words fell from his lips.

'We got our own problems to fret about, Tan.'

Gibson pulled on his reins and began to lead the exhausted pinto back down the narrow canyon. Rainbow remained at his side as they walked back to the spot where they had first heard the sound of the thundering mustangs.

When they eventually reached Rainbow's fallen mount, neither man would care for the sight which greeted them. For when several thousand head of stampeding horseflesh trample over anything lying on the ground, little remains except a bloody mess bearing

no resemblance to what it had once
been.

It was a chilling reminder of what
could still happen to them should their
luck finally run out.

10

Marshal Vincent and his deputy Ericson had not remained long in Ravens Creek. Theirs was a pressing engagement which both men were determined to honour. They had been following the notorious Brody gang too long to waste time in meaningless places such as the bawdy Ravens Creek. After consuming steak and black-eyed beans plus a pot of strong coffee, the two lawmen were ready to continue their mission. Ready to place the final piece of the jigsaw puzzle into place.

Knowing their own horses were spent and not up to the hard ride ahead, they had purchased fresh mounts. Vincent bought enough ammunition to cover any unforeseen occurrences whilst Ericson had ensured they had enough provisions before they set out again on their quest.

The two men had studied their brand new map whilst eating the meal provided by the mayor. Neither man had spoken more than a handful of words to the town official as he tried to cajole them into staying in Ravens Creek. They had just eaten their food and drunk their coffee as the older man had pleaded for them to remain in his town.

But no words could deflect either man from his chosen plan of action. They had studied the map and knew exactly what their next course of action would be.

To them, there was no alternative.

They had the scent of their targets in their nostrils and nothing could make them change their minds.

Mayor McBride had tried to tell the tall pair of law officers that they had no chance of catching up with the notorious Cole Brody and his followers. They had left Ravens Creek roughly three weeks earlier and even on fresh horses, the marshal and his deputy could never reduce that sort of lead.

But Vincent and Ericson were no ordinary lawmen content to blindly chase their prey. They had a plan which would reduce the distance between themselves and the Brody gang. For these riders were unlike most who travelled through the barren wastes of the scorched desolate territories. They knew exactly how to use the land itself and how to get from one place to another in the fastest possible way.

Marshal Vincent led the way atop his fresh mount, with Ericson dutifully riding a few paces behind. They were not using the established trail which Cole Brody and his band of lethal followers had taken for Pueblo Flats, but heading towards the distant newly opened railroad that they knew lay a mere twenty miles east of the liquor-soaked township of Ravens Creek. A railroad spur had been laid to take fresh cattle from remote ranches to the eager agents in the east, avoiding trail drives across the treacherous parched land between.

Marshal Vincent knew that only one small town lay in the direction in which Cole Brody had headed. Why he was taking his band of ruthless killers to Pueblo Flats, the marshal could only speculate, but he was not about to waste time following the trail. The railroad avoided all the natural obstacles and headed in a direct line across the barren wastes.

It was a long shot, but Vincent knew that if they were fortunate enough to flag down a southbound locomotive, they could cut their journey down from nine days to a mere twenty-four hours. For the newly opened railtrack spur went within ten miles of the remote Pueblo Flats. From there, he and his deputy would have an easy ride to the place where he was convinced Cole Brody and his gang were headed.

It was indeed a long shot but Vincent had lived his life playing such odds.

Riding across a huge sand dune, the

pair of law officers suddenly saw something below them. At first it appeared to be alive as its light danced in their weary eyes. Then, as they rode closer, it was obvious what it was that was catching the rays of the blistering sun.

Reining in their mounts as they stared down at the gleaming iron railtracks before them, Vincent began to smile at his partner.

Soon Ericson would know why the usually emotionless marshal was smiling so broadly. It was indeed a rare occurrence. Then the deputy marshal also heard the noise in the distance. It was the distinctive sound of a heavily burdened locomotive heading towards them.

'I guess we are a tad lucky that the train is coming along right now, Marshal,' Ericson sighed.

Vincent reached back to his saddle-bags, produced two large flares and ignited them both. Tossing one to either side of the tracks he waited until the train was in sight.

The whistle from the labouring engine echoed around the desolate landscape. Vincent could see the heads of the engineer and his mate leaning out from their cab as they began to apply the brakes.

'Luck ain't got nothing to do with it.'

'They seen us, Marshal,' Ericson said.

'And they're slowing down to a stop,' Vincent added.

'I still think we're lucky, Marshal,' Ericson repeated as he stared hard at his superior who was thumbing a small grubby booklet in his hands. 'What you got there?'

'The timetable, Deputy.'

'So you knew exactly when the damn train was due.' Ericson shook his head. 'I thought we was just lucky getting here at the same time as the train turned up.'

Marshal Vincent pocketed the booklet and then dismounted from his horse. He held tightly on to his reins as the smoke poured off the flares and the huge locomotive ground to a halt amid a flurry of hisses.

'Smart men make their own luck.'

11

It was carnage. There was no other word which could adequately describe it. It was written across the churned-up sand, in the blood of the mustang men. A mysterious silence once again enveloped this place where only minutes earlier there had been a deafening deadly eruption of chilling noise. The two large covered wagons had managed to remain upright and withstand the sudden arrival of more than a thousand head of wild galloping mustangs. Yet there had also been living men in this dry sun-baked place. Gibson's men.

Some of whom had not fared as well as the pair of prairie schooners. For two of the wranglers, death had chosen them to ride a higher more peaceful trail.

What remained of the bodies of Joe Green and the young Sol Dane were scattered across the dry ground. They, unlike their fellow mustang-hunters, had not managed to get beneath the flat-bed bodies of the prairie schooners in time. They had been stranded a mere fifty feet from the small barricade of two vehicles against the canyon wall, when the wild horses had suddenly emerged from one of the countless canyons.

No man, however fleet of foot could outrun stampeding mustangs. It had been a simple fact which both Joe Green and Sol Dane had learned to their cost. Yet they had not had any alternative when the flared nostrils of the rampaging horses had appeared. The two men knew that to remain where they were against the sand-coloured rockface offered only the certainty of death by crushing hoofs. Sol Dane had started to run for the wagons first with the older, slower Joe Green on his heels.

It had all happened so quickly. There had been little warning to alert any of

Tan Gibson's team as they patiently awaited his and Rainbow's return.

What had at first seemed like distant thunder rolling angrily over the maze of canyons, had indeed been the approaching black stallion and his herd of countless mustangs converging on the wranglers' small camp.

It had been a brutal lesson to all five of the experienced horsemen. One which would cost two of them their very lives.

Fred Scott, Rufas Blake and Keno Smith still huddled together beneath the larger of the wagons, trying to come to terms with the loss of their two friends.

The crusty old-timer Fred Scott had seen numerous herds of wild horses before but never set eyes upon any as large as the one which had suddenly appeared and torn through this sweltering hell-hole.

He rubbed his whiskers and gazed out to where he had last seen the blond youngster, Dane. The kid had been running towards the wagons as the herd of mustangs bore down on them. Scott had never seen such terror etched on the face of anyone, the way it was carved into Sol Dane's.

Fred Scott had witnessed many deaths in his long life but this one was the most cruel and the most unexpected.

Rufas Blake lay next to Fred Scott. For the first time since he had first encountered the older man he was not talking about his own imaginary illnesses. For he had seen the herd of wild horses appearing from the mouth of one of the many canyons and thrown himself beneath the closer of the covered wagons. He had rolled in the hot sand only seconds before the black stallion had led his herd crashing into the tall wooden vehicles. He had spotted Joe Green vainly attempting to run back to the relative safety of the roped-together wagons. Rufas Blake was still shaking in shock as his memory kept filling his mind with the image of the hapless wrangler being crushed beneath the hoofs of the rampaging horses.

The bragging Keno Smith had not managed to open his mouth since the incident. He had not seen either of his less fortunate companions meet their deaths, but he had heard their pitiful screams as they were crushed beneath the unshod hoofs. It was something that still echoed in his shocked brain.

Their haunting terror-filled screams!

What was this place that their leader Tan Gibson had brought them to?

It was a question each of the survivors asked themselves as they lay silently under the wagons. The ground still shook beneath their bellies as the echoes of the massive herd vibrated in the very bedrock itself.

What were they doing here?

Somehow, Fred Scott managed to raise himself on to all fours and crawled to where their cutting horses and wagon-teams were secured by many expertly tied ropes. He looked up into the eyes of the animals and then moved cautiously back to his two companions. There was a fire in the eyes of their horses. A fire which was born out of horror.

Scott sat with his spine against the large wheel and produced his tobacco-pouch from his shirt. With trembling fingers he managed to roll himself a cigarette as he listened to their own horses snorting.

'We ought to leave our horses be for a while, boys,' Scott suggested as he placed the thin smoke between his dry lips and searched for a match.

'Why?' Keno asked.

'They got fear in their craws!' Scott explained, striking a match along the metal wheel-hoop.

Rufas Blake crawled next to the older man.

'You mean them mustangs have managed to spook our horses, old man?' Keno asked.

'Yep! That's exactly what I mean,

Keno,' Scott said through a mouthful of smoke.

Keno glanced up from beneath the wagon at the firmly secured horses between the wooden vehicles and the almost sheer canyon wall. The old man was right, he thought. There was fear in the eyes of every one of their animals as they chafed against their restraints. Perhaps they had felt their own wild hearts tearing inside them as the mustangs tore into the clearing and surged past the wagons. Whatever the truth of it was, every one of the creatures was now as dangerous as those that had claimed the lives of Joe Green and the young Sol.

'They are sure lathered up, Fred,' Keno admitted reluctantly.

'Only a fool would go near them horses when they are all fired up like that that,' Scott added.

'Reckon so.'

'I'm willing to stay here until Rainbow and Tan get back,' Rufas said quietly.

Keno Smith stared across to where he had last seen Tan Gibson and Rainbow riding earlier that morning. It was the same canyon that the massive herd had suddenly emerged from. Even his tired mind knew that two horsemen riding straight into the onrush of such a massive herd of stampeding mustangs, coming in the opposite direction, had little chance of survival.

'You figure Tan and Rainbow are still alive, Fred?'

Fred Scott sucked on his smoke and did not reply. None of the trio wished to speculate further. There seemed only one answer and none of them cared for it.

12

There was a feeling of solemn inevitability within the hearts of the three tanned figures. Could it be that they alone amongst the citizens of Pueblo Flats knew something that everyone else did not? Or were they allowing their own vivid imaginations to run wild simply because they had grown paranoid about their town's secret wealth? Had greed finally corrupted the elderly trio into seeing threats where none actually existed? Judge Bevis Hogan, Arthur Bearcutt and Marvin Caine knew there was still time for their entire community to flee, yet it seemed that every other person within Pueblo Flats did not share their vision of impending doom.

What seemed so real to Hogan and his two friends appeared nothing more than the workings of over zealous minds to the rest of their small community.

Few within the town gave a damn that the drunken wretch they had sent to Ravens Creek with their gold dust had not yet returned. Most hoped he had fallen off his horse and broken his worthless neck. The loss of a few bags of gold dust meant nothing to the people of Pueblo Flats. Why should it? They had far more gold dust in their small bank than most large city banks could ever dream of possessing.

The loss of a few bags meant nothing.

All the concerned words from the three men who had slept little for days, meant absolutely nothing to the complacent residents of the sun-bleached town. Strangers rarely visited Pueblo Flats through choice. What sane person would ride into the middle of virtual desert when there were so many lush fertile alternatives to attract them? The people of the small rich town could not understand Judge Hogan's concern.

It was irrational.

They simply could not imagine anyone venturing out into the tinder-dry wilderness and heading for their tiny town on the vague chance there might be gold there.

After several hours of passionate talking falling on deaf ears, even Bearcutt, Hogan and Caine had begun to wonder if their fears were indeed justified or simply senseless worrying.

The town had mocked them. For with shared wealth beyond the wildest imaginings of ordinary folks, none of Pueblo Flats' people seemed capable of stretching their thoughts beyond the town's boundaries.

It did seem irrational. Just because their messenger had not returned to the fold on time, it was something of a huge leap to imagine that he had told some unknown ruthless outlaw about the unimaginable wealth waiting to be harvested by the first passing gang.

Yet however ludicrous it sounded, it was gnawing at the craws of the three elderly men. Judge Bevis Hogan finally admitted defeat in trying to get the rest of Pueblo Flats to even consider his concern. Turning away from the sanctimonious faces he wandered out of the saloon with his two best friends into the blinding sunshine again. The thinly disguised laughter echoed in each of the three men's ears with every step they took across the white-hot street.

They had sipped the finest whiskey during the long wearying talk with all the adult members of their unique community. Yet the women had voiced their opinions the loudest as usual, drowning out the less able voices of their menfolk. Over the years it seemed as if the women of Pueblo Flats had managed to drain the last vestiges of masculinity from their husbands.

The three men approached the livery stables slowly and each, unbeknownst to the others, was thankful that they alone within the small town no longer had any mate to stop them speaking their minds or being men.

The domineering females of Pueblo

Flats tended to be less imaginative than their liquor-drinking male counterparts. Less willing to see something beyond the horizon until it actually presented itself.

It was a character flaw that might just prove to be fatal.

The judge felt as if he and his two friends had been made to look like drunken cowards by the women of their town. Made to look as if they were afraid of their own shadows.

Hogan did not like the taste it left in his dry mouth as he rested an arm upon the fence pole of the small livery stable and stared at the half-dozen horses which roamed around within its paddock.

There was little use for horses in Pueblo Flats as few of its people ever went anywhere. Apart from the nearby canyons with their towering rocky spires, there was nothing much to see outside the confines of the small town beside the unassuming river. The six horses were jointly owned by the town and only used whenever one of their number was chosen to ride to a distant town to exchange their precious gold dust for hard cash and provisions.

'What ya thinking about, Judge?' Bearcutt asked as he produced an unopened bottle of whiskey from the bib of his overalls.

'The humiliation that those damn women have poured over us, Arthur,' Hogan replied.

'Was kinda like a barrel of molasses,' Caine agreed, watching Bearcutt pulling the cork from the neck of the bottle.

'I'm sure glad my wife up and died before she got like the rest of them witches,' Hogan added.

'Women sure like to belittle men,' Caine grumbled.

'We could be right about us being in danger,' Bearcutt said before raising the bottle to his lips and taking a single swallow. It tasted good.

Judge Bevis Hogan knew that their fears might be correct even if the rest of the town thought otherwise. It only took one loud mouth to spill the beans about their secret wealth to bring every sort of vermin down upon them.

'Why didn't none of the other men listen to us, Judge?' Caine asked as he accepted the bottle from Bearcutt.

'Why? Because their damn women wouldn't let them,' Hogan snarled through gritted teeth. 'They've become spineless. Women do that to a man after a while. It's a sort of sickness they develop after they lose their looks or their shape. Or both.'

'I'm plumb glad I never got hitched.' Caine coughed before rubbing his mouth across the back of his sleeve. The whiskey burned its way down his throat as he handed the bottle to the judge. 'Reckon them fivedollar whores over in Ravens Creek have their uses. Leastways, after you've had your fun, you can leave them be.'

'Women are evil when they got ya hooked.' Hogan swilled the amber liquor down his neck before returning the bottle to Bearcutt.

'Ain't no reason to the critters.'

'We are right, boys!' Hogan snorted.

'We could be, Judge. I've got me a feeling in my innards that we are.'

'I mean we are right to be fretting. For all we know there are bandits or gold-diggers heading this way right now. Men who'll find Pueblo Flats a ripe apple to pluck.' Hogan stared hard at the horses within the paddock before them.

'How will we ever know?' Caine rubbed the sweat off his eyebrows and rested both his arms on the top pole of the fence.

'We won't unless we saddle up three of them horses and take us a ride, Marve.' Hogan was grinning.

'You mean we head for Ravens Creek?' Bearcutt frowned.

'Yep. That way we'll either meet our long-lost friend on the trail or someone else lurking out there.'

Caine sighed heavily. 'It might be dangerous.'

'Not as dangerous as it'll be if'n we

just sit here like the women and wait for trouble to arrive.' Bevis Hogan could feel the sap rising inside his veins. It had been a long time since he had felt so exhilarated. He knew whatever was out there on the dry dusty trail between his town and the distant Ravens Creek, it could not be worse than the cruel jibes of frustrated females.

'Then it'll be too late to do anything.' Bearcutt nodded.

'Get some guns and ammunition. I'll saddle up the horses.'

13

Tan Gibson had managed to find the canteens amid the blood and gore which had once been Rainbow's prized cutting horse. They needed all the canteens they could find once they located the water-hole which the mustangs regularly visited. It was a long ride back to their wagons and fellow mustang-men. Gibson knew that their very existence might depend upon a single mouthful of the precious liquid they so desperately sought.

'We sure are in a real mess, Tan.' Rainbow sighed as he walked beside the grim-faced wrangler who led his pinto on and on with singular determination.

'We've been in worse spots than this, Rainbow.'

'We have? Funny, I can't recall one quite as bad as this.'

Gibson pulled the brim of his Stetson

down over his eyes and glanced in his friend's direction.

'What about that time we was in Laredo?'

'Oh yeah. I'd forgotten about that.' Rainbow forced a smile and continued keeping pace with the man who had far longer legs than himself. It was no easy matter staying level with a man whose stride was so much greater, but he tried.

After walking for nearly an hour, both men noticed the ears of the pinto prick. The animal began to snort and tug at the reins in Tan Gibson's hands.

'What is it? What's wrong with him?' Rainbow asked as he jumped away from the skittish animal.

'Reckon he can smell something, Rainbow,' Gibson replied.

Finally Gibson released his grip and allowed the horse to run away from himself and his exhausted pal. Both men watched with tired eyes as the horse galloped on ahead and around a gigantic wall of solid rock.

'What ya let the pinto go for, Tan?' Rainbow gasped as he staggered to the side of Gibson.

'He ain't gone far.'

'What ya mean?'

'Can't you smell it?'

Rainbow sniffed at the air.

'Water?'

'Yep, it's water all right, Rainbow.' Gibson rubbed his face with the palm of his hand and sighed heavily.

Both men began somehow to increase their pace as they stumbled along the floor of the narrow canyon. They did not have to go far before seeing a sight which amazed them both.

Rounding the corner where they had lost sight of the fleeing pinto, they suddenly saw something which filled them both with total amazement. It was indeed water, but not a mere creek or even a river.

This was far bigger than that.

This was a lake. A lake surrounded by lush vegetation. No wonder the herd of mustangs stayed within this otherwise deadly place, Gibson thought. Where else in this dry country could they find anything remotely similar to this veritable oasis?

'Do you see what I think I see, Rainbow?' Gibson blinked hard as he tried to convince himself he was not facing a mirage.

'I could be dreaming.'

'Then we are both having the same dream, partner.'

'Are my eyes telling me lies, Tan?' Rainbow asked as he staggered along beside the taller man towards the vast expanse of water.

'I see water. A lotta water, Rainbow.'

'So do I, Tan.'

Gibson took hold of his friend's elbow and continued walking towards the sweet fresh-smelling lake. He stared with burning eyes at the grass and flowers which filled every spare inch of ground within the massive clearing. It could have been a mirage but was it possible for two men to witness the same mirage at the same time?

Gibson thought not.

This had to be real, but how could it be real?

It made no sense. None at all.

Then Gibson spotted something high up on one of the sand-coloured cliff walls. It was a cave opening by all appearances, but water flowed from it and ran down the surface of the rockface until it reached the floor of the canyon. There it continuously filled the lake.

Rainbow fell on to his knees and dropped his head into the cool fresh water. It was the longest drink he had ever taken and each precious drop was savoured as if it were the most expensive imported French wine.

Tan Gibson knelt, scooped up some of the water and wet his lips. He studied the luxuriant area with cautious disbelieving eyes. As the pure water trickled down his dry throat, Gibson began to realize that this was no mirage.

Then the sound of a distant shot rang out. Gibson stood with water trailing down his face as he listened to the echo bouncing off the walls about them.

'Where did that come from, Tan?' Rainbow asked as he got back to his feet.

Gibson said nothing as his keen eyes searched the very top of the mountainous canyon walls. He knew that somewhere up there, high above them, someone had a gun and was using it.

He wondered who and why.

14

It was a few hours past noon when the bullet shot from Lance Parker's pistol awoke his dozing fellow gang-members. The sun was starting to make its way back down towards the western horizon, casting its long black shadows across the outlaws' temporary encampment. Yet there seemed to be no reduction in the scorching temperature which tortured both the men and beasts of the Brody gang.

Eleven sets of eyes flashed in the direction of Parker as he twirled his smoking six-shooter. These were men who were not happy at being in this godforsaken place and even less so at being disturbed by the sound of a bullet. They had eaten their ration of beans and jerky and used up the last of their coffee-grounds before closing their eyes to rest. They knew they were close to a town where they could acquire more provisions, but none of the men liked the idea of tipping off the residents of Pueblo Flats of their imminent arrival. Cole Brody was the least happy about the ear-splitting gunshot.

The hooded eyes of the sixty-year-old Cole Brody flashed like daggers across the expanse of sand between them. It had been a long time since any of his gang had seen their leader looking so furious.

Rising to his feet and dusting himself off, Brody stared around his resting men until he spotted the gun in the outlaw's hand.

'Parker!' shouted Cole Brody, moving across the white sand until he was standing above the thin sneering form of Lance Parker. The stout outlaw leader glared down at the smoking pistol in Parker's gloved hand.

'What's wrong, Cole? Did I wake ya?' Parker grinned as he toyed with the weapon.

Brody kicked the seated outlaw hard enough for the man to yelp like an injured animal.

'Did that wake you?'

'Aaargh!' Parker reeled sideways in agony as the pointed cowboy boot was withdrawn before slamming into him again.

'Starting to get the point, Parker?' Cole Brody spat.

Parker was probably less than half Brody's age and had long resented the fact that he was subservient to a fat old man.

'What's eating at you, Cole?'

'You probably woke up every damn critter this side of the Rio Grande with that shot, Parker,' Brody seethed, resting the palm of his hand on the butt of his own pistol.

'I don't like hanging around doing nothing, Cole.' Parker rubbed his bruised leg.

Brody snatched the gun from the man's hand angrily and jabbed its barrel into Parker's temple. A trickle of blood trailed down the scarred face.

'You darn fool. That shot could have been heard over ten miles away.' Cole Brody waved the pistol in front of Parker's face as he shouted at the wincing man.

Parker staggered to his feet and growled at the older man.

'So what? What you scared of?'

Without a second's hesitation, Cole Brody whipped the barrel of the pistol across the unshaven face, sending Parker crashing back down on to the ground. Blood spurted from the cruel gash on his cheek down over the dusty shirt-front.

'Quit hitting me, old man!' Parker pleaded.

'You mindless bastard. I want to ride into Pueblo Flats after sundown unannounced. We don't want them knowing that we are coming to rob them, do we?'

'What difference will it make?' Parker asked as he mopped the blood dripping from his face with his sleeve. 'I figure them folks are just a bunch of fat farmers.'

'I don't want us to ride into no ambush, boy!' Cole Brody was not the biggest of men but he had a power far beyond his height. He hovered over the younger outlaw like a diamond-back rattler waiting to strike.

Lance Parker cast his eyes around the faces of the ten other men seated around the remnants of their camp-fire. Each of them was glaring angrily in his direction. They too knew it did not pay to advertise one's presence to the inhabitants of any town, no matter how small. Even hick farmers could set an ambush capable of thinning down the most experienced of outlaw gangs.

Parker spat the blood from his mouth before replying;

'I was just a mite bored, Cole. We should never have come here to this place. I don't like it.'

'You'll change your tune if we find that gold in Pueblo Flats.' Cole Brody began to relax as he remembered the words which had dripped from the mouth of the drunken sop back in Ravens Creek. Gold enough to make every one of his gang rich beyond their wildest dreams.

'What if there ain't no gold?'

'You better start praying that there is, Parker!'

'He's had enough, Cole,' the outlaw known only as Jones mumbled.

'If any of our boys get themselves shot tonight, they'll know exactly who to blame, Parker!' Brody snarled as he tossed the gun between the outlaw's legs.

Sheepishly, Lance Parker picked up his gun and slid it back into its holster.

'I'm sorry, Cole. I didn't think.'

'Shut the hell up.' The rotund figure of Cole Brody strode confidently into the centre of his seated men and lowered his head until his eyes seemed to be twice their normal size.

'Break camp, boys. We got us a town to visit.'

Smoke billowed black and dense from the tall chimneystack of the train and hung on the thin hot air. The massive locomotive thundered along its gleaming new rails at a speed rarely achieved by other trains. There was a very good reason for this; it was all downhill.

Pulling ten stock-cars filled with prime white-face and longhorn steers, plus a flat car and guard's coach, the train was increasing its speed with every passing minute. The gradient had been well considered by the railroad company when they had designed this spur line. It used every incline the desolate landscape had to offer. It made perfect sense to the two lawmen as they stood next to their tethered horses on the flat car. The train went uphill when empty heading west and downhill when returning filled with stock towards the east.

The two lawmen had remained standing for the entire journey and showed no signs of succumbing to the tiredness they both felt so deeply. It was as if they feared sleep. Dreams brought memories better left alone. For dreams could not be controlled, even by the strongest-willed of men.

Marshal Vincent stared out into the dusty canyons below the high railtrack and sucked on a thin black cigar as the train hurtled on towards its destination. Smoke drifted from his mouth slowly as he brooded and planned.

His mind could think of only one thing and that was catching up with Cole Brody and his followers. It was a thought which filled his every waking moment.

For three years they had hunted Cole Brody.

Yet this was no ordinary chase for the experienced marshal and his faithful deputy. This was far more personal than that. He had hunted the infamous Brody gang for three long years without ever deviating from his chosen task. Ericson had been with him every step of the way because he too was driven by something more than just a desire to administer the law.

For both the determined lawmen had lost those closest to them at the hands of Cole Brody and his brothers and their bloody followers.

Marshal Vincent still recalled the moment back at Dodge when he had discovered the bodies of his wife and child after they had been killed by the infamous Brodys. Ericson had discovered his parents slaughtered with equal brutality. They had been out of town on their regular rounds when the gang had struck. The Brody gang had robbed the local Wells Fargo offices before terrorizing the entire community. There had been more than twenty of them back then. Men bent on destruction and getting whatever they wanted, no matter what the cost in human life was. Locals in the town had told Vincent and Ericson how the Brody brothers had deliberately asked where the marshal lived. Perhaps they had not managed to steal enough money that day and wanted to take their anger out on the loved ones of the law. Whatever the reason for the carnage, it had destroyed the lives of two honest men and turned them into ghosts of their former selves. Turned them into nothing more than hunters bent on revenge.

The cars of the long train rocked from side to side as it sped ever onward, with the two grim-faced men standing close to one another yet seldom speaking.

Theirs was an understanding born out of mutual hatred for the vermin they hunted. They did not have to question one another as to the rights or wrongs of what they did. To them, there was simply no other way. They had to catch up with the hideous outlaws who had mercilessly slain their families three years earlier.

An eye for an eye. It was as simple as that.

Ericson knew he would be at his partner's side the moment they finally caught up with the gang. They would stand shoulder to shoulder and kill or be killed because that was the only justice the outlaws deserved. There would be no trial for Brody or his followers. No lawyers to twist the facts and make a jury so confused that they would release the gang to commit more and more outrages.

Cole Brody would face their guns. Then only God would have a say in who survived or fell into the dust.

Vincent allowed the breeze to remove the grey ash from the tip of his cigar as he soothed his nervous mount. He looked at his deputy and both men seemed to read each other's minds. They nodded, as if agreeing to words which had not been spoken, only thought.

Vincent knew they were going to finally catch up with Cole Brody this time, because the stout outlaw had at long last made a mistake.

Cole Brody had abandoned his normal caution this time and headed deep into a land where only sand and thirst reigned supreme. A land he had no knowledge of. Why he had chosen to lead his gang towards the remote township of Pueblo Flats, neither lawman knew or cared. Brody had finally made a mistake and the marshal and deputy marshal were determined to capitalize upon it.

For three years they had hunted the cunning outlaw from one town to another. Always arriving weeks after Brody and his gang had departed. Over those three long years the pair of lawmen had seen the gang diminish in size as one by one they were whittled away.

Yet Vincent and Ericson continued following.

This time vengeance would be theirs.

15

It had taken a while for the teams of wagon-horses to calm down enough for the three surviving members of Tan Gibson's crew to risk hitching them up. The highly trained cutting mounts had settled down much faster, but even they remained nervous. It was as if they knew the black stallion and his herd of mustangs would return. The only question was: when?

The three wranglers had worked quickly getting the animals saddled and back in harness. Each of the trio knew they had to use speed because it was the only thing they still had going for them. They had to get away from this place as fast as possible just in case the mustangs returned.

Each of the men doubted their covered wagons could withstand a second battering by the wild horseflesh that roamed these canyons.

The two prairie schooners were barely able to negotiate the narrow twisting canyon, but they did. There was no other choice once they entered the long seemingly endless route between the walls of sand-rock. There was no place to turn the vehicles, so they had to continue on and on until they reached the end. It was not a journey that Scott, Blake or Smith relished but the only one that offered hope.

For that was all they had left, a thin scraping of hope.

It was a wary Fred Scott who sat high on his driver's seat and nursed his six-horse team carefully onward at the head of their now smaller outfit. Rufas Blake expertly followed in his wagon as Keno Smith rode his cutting horse and led the pair of mounts belonging to their dead comrades.

They had not buried the young Sol Kane or the skilful Joe Green before hastily leaving the clearing. There had been no time for such civilized things. No time to do anything except hightail it out of that dangerous sun-drenched place. Besides, each of them secretly knew in is heart that it was impossible to bury mere fragments of men, and that was all that was left of their two dead companions.

Thousands of merciless hoofs leave little in their wake except bloodstained sand.

The wranglers had decided between them that they had three options. The first was to stay put and wait for the massive herd of mustangs to return. This offered the risk of them losing even more of their depleted crew.

The second choice was to turn tail and try to head back out of the deep valley of countless canyons. To take this option was to write Tan Gibson and Rainbow off for dead. Something none of them felt able to do with any certainty.

The third choice which presented itself to the minds of the trio of mustang men was to hitch up the wagons and venture into the canyon where they had last seen their friends entering.

The first two courses of action seemed less risky than the third but meant they would not replenish their dwindling supply of water.

Heading after Rainbow and Gibson at least offered them a chance of discovering water. The herd of wild horses did not gallop in and out of that narrow canyon for exercise alone. The three men knew that horses could smell water miles off and, if nothing else, they might find enough to fill their almost dry barrels.

The three wranglers could no longer see the sun above the rugged canyon spires and knew the day was quickly coming to an end. They had no idea how much time they still had before darkness made their trek even more difficult, but as long as there was some light entering the canyon, they would continue forging on.

As Fred Scott cracked his sixteen-foot-long bullwhip over the heads of his team, he suddenly noticed something ahead in the shadows. Squinting with eyes long past their best, he focused on the figures as his wagon drew closer.

For a moment the wily old-timer was uncertain that he was actually seeing Tan Gibson and Rainbow. He allowed his team of horses to venture another thirty feet before ramming his right leg down on the long brake-pole.

Scott's scream of delight echoed around the highwalled canyon long after the two wranglers had reached the front wheel of his wagon.

'We thought you was dead, boys!' Scott exclaimed.

'Nearly was, old man,' Gibson retorted.

'Find the water hole?'

'You better believe it!' Rainbow forced a grin as he noticed Gibson staring hard at the pair of horses being led by Keno Smith.

Tan Gibson leaned on the brake-pole

of Scott's wagon and watched as Rufas Blake clambered down from the second wagon and approached. Then the mustang man returned his attention to Keno Smith riding slowly through the gap between the large vehicles and the canyon wall with the pair of saddled horses in tow.

'Where's Sol and Joe, Fred?'

Fred Scott shook his head sorrowfully as the horror of what had occurred earlier flooded back into his tired mind.

'Dead, Tan. They both got themselves killed.'

Gibson swallowed hard as Rainbow rested a hand on the nose of Keno's mount.

'The mustangs get them?'

'They nearly got all of us, Tan,' Rufas Blake added with a voice shaking in a mixture of tiredness and fear.

'Never seen the like of it before,' Keno Smith said before dismounting.

'Must have been at least a thousand of the critters.' Fred Scott sniffed emotionally as he stared down at his fellow wranglers. 'I seen me a lot of mustangs before, but none like them. They were damn killers, Tan. They seemed to want to kill Sol and Joe.'

'That black stallion sure looks an ornery cuss, and no mistake,' Gibson said. 'He almost put paid to me and Rainbow.'

'We thought you and Rainbow must be goners too.' Blake cleared his throat. 'The way that herd came thundering out of this canyon with their nostrils flaring, we figured they must have killed you boys for certain.'

Gibson looked around the faces of his men.

'They almost did, boys. They almost did.'

⋆   ⋆   ⋆

The wagons were positioned across the narrow mouth of the fertile oasis canyon as Tan Gibson and his men began the back-breaking chore of filling the huge water-barrels strapped securely to their wagons' frames.

It was something they did with a zeal that only men who have experienced true thirst would enjoy. The sheer pleasure of handling wet buckets was soothing to the blistered, sunburned hands of each of the five wranglers. Bucket after bucket was carried from the lake to the large barrels and poured into their cavernous bellies.

'How come we blocked up the entrance to this place, Tan?' Keno asked, curious, as they replaced the wooden lids back on top of the last barrel.

'I reckon them mustangs are gonna get a mite confused if we can stop them reaching the lake, Keno,' Gibson replied.

'But what good will that do us?'

Gibson squatted down on the ground and ran his fingers through his hair as he stared at the lush vegetation before them.

'Them mustangs are like spoiled brats. They roam these canyons freely getting their fill of the grass and water in this place. I figure this is the only reason they've managed to stay alive in this damn maze of dry canyons. If we can stop them getting to the water and the sweet grass for a couple of days, they'll lose their arrogance. They'll be thirsty like we were. They'll be a lot easier to catch.'

Fred Scott stopped above the seated wrangler.

'That sounds like a darn good idea, Tan.'

'Pretty smart,' Blake added.

'If these wagons can hold up against that much horseflesh pounding on them.' Rainbow sighed.

Gibson got back to his feet and studied the large wooden vehicles with a keen eye. They were solid enough but perhaps Rainbow was right. What if they could not stand up to being charged into by countless galloping mustangs?

'We better get the ropes and hog-tie these wagons together, boys,' Gibson said. 'Rainbow could be right. We better try and make sure he ain't.'

As the men worked feverishly with their ropes, the stars slowly began to appear in the quickly darkening sky above their heads. Yet even as the blinding light of day faded from this strange place, there was no noticeable drop in the baking heat which filled the humid oasis.

Tan Gibson rested his knuckles on his gunbelt and looked up at the rocks bathed in moonlight which towered all around them. It was like being corralled in some gigantic hole created by a power far beyond their understanding.

'Reckon we're stuck in this place, Tan,' Fred Scott muttered as he removed his store-bought teeth and knelt down by the pure water of the lake.

Gibson glanced down and watched the old-timer rinsing the teeth in the water before returning them to his mouth.

'We ain't trapped, Fred.'

'We ain't?' Scott said as he straightened up beside the younger man.

'Nope. There's a trail out of here.' Gibson pointed to their right.

'I don't see nothing, boy.'

'It's there OK. I spotted it before you boys showed up. It leads all the way to the top of them cliffs.' Tan Gibson rubbed his chin.

'How wide?'

'Wide enough for a cautious horse to navigate,' Gibson replied.

'We couldn't drive no herd of mustangs up a trail like that, could we?' Fred Scott was wondering why Gibson was so interested in the trail if they could not use it to their advantage.

'I wasn't figuring on driving no mustangs up there, Fred,' Tan Gibson said. 'But an hour or so back, me and Rainbow heard us a shot coming from up there. I'm a mite curious.'

16

The three riders were not expert horsemen by any yardstick one wished to measure them by. Judge Bevis Hogan had seldom thrown his leg across a wide Texan saddle during his many years and it showed as he steered the skittish mount beneath his ample rump across the dark sea of sand. Yet even his own discomfort could not sway him from his chosen crusade.

Marvin Caine was less incompetent, yet far from at ease as he rode beside the judge. He continually checked and rechecked the weaponry strapped to his waist as he rode. For over his thirty-two years of existence, he had never actually fired a pistol in anger. Caine had used a squirrel-gun once but not hit his target or anything else for that matter and had managed to keep his ineptitude with firearms a secret ever since. He wondered if his two riding companions were better shots than he. They had to be, he continually reassured himself. How could they be worse?

Only Arthur Bearcutt seemed at home atop his chosen horse as he rode slightly ahead of the other two riders. He had once been a man who regularly used a rifle for hunting but that had been long ago. A different time and a different place. The land around Pueblo Flats offered little game worthy of killing, let alone putting in a cooking-pot. Bearcutt rode with a doubt in his mind as to his own abilities. Was it possible to retain a skill with a rifle if you had not even fired one in over two decades?

The three men had ignored the mocking jibes of their fellow Pueblo Flats citizens and ridden out of the remote township towards the unknown.

The riders had a feeling that they would find the answers they sought out beyond the horizon. Answers that would not only prove them correct but also make everyone in Pueblo Flats who had ridiculed them, take stock.

Judge Bevis Hogan had not been able to eat properly for nearly three days. His guts were twisted in fear that at long last their secret wealth had finally become common knowledge in the outlying towns. The judge held tightly on to his reins, the way men who have no understanding of horses do. Yet he remained high in his saddle for nearly eight long miles beside the other two riders as they headed out into the star-filled desolation.

The three men continued to pass the bottle of fine sipping whisky between them as they continued along the trail which they knew led to the distant Ravens Creek. None of the riders were even close to being drunk, but they were indeed now devoid of any of the trepidation that had been with them during the beginning of their journey.

The sky above them had turned from the brightest blue to the deepest black over the past hour of their quest. They knew they would find answers if they just managed to remain in their saddles and on course.

The answers were out there somewhere.

Hogan toyed with the unaccustomed spurs he had attached to his boots. Jabbing the horse on and on, Hogan somehow remained in his uncomfortable saddle and kept pace with the pair of riders beside him.

Suddenly, Bearcutt reined his horse in.

'You see that?'

His friends stopped their own mounts and stared across the now flat landscape now illuminated by the bright moon. For a while neither Hogan or Caine could focus on what the shaking finger of Bearcutt was aiming at. Then they began to understand why the tone of the bearded man's voice was riddled with concern.

Moonlight bounced off the dozen riders as they came closer and closer.

'I see them,' Judge Hogan said in a

faltering voice as he reached to his side and drew out his Colt. He rested it in his lap behind the horn of his saddle.

'This ain't right,' Caine yelped like a kicked hound. 'I didn't figure on there being so many of them.'

'I count an even dozen, Judge.' Arthur Bearcutt tossed the empty whisky bottle away, reached for his rifle and withdrew it from its long leather scabbard.

'Yep. There are twelve of the bastards OK,' Hogan confirmed.

'Who do you reckon they are?' Bearcutt pulled the trigger back on his rifle until it locked into place.

'They ain't preachers, and that's for sure,' Judge Hogan said drily.

'I don't like this, Judge,' Caine said as he rubbed the spittle from the corners of his mouth.

'Easy, Marve. There ain't no call to get scared.' Bearcutt snorted as he watched the riders getting closer and closer to them.

'I didn't figure on us riding into no dozen men.' Caine's voice was now pitched just shy of total panic. 'I ain't keen on facing up to them *hombres.*'

Judge Hogan glanced at the youngest member of their small band and was troubled by the sight. He had never taken Caine for a coward in all the years he had known him. Until now.

'We gotta stand firm, Marve. We have to face these strangers together like men.'

Marvin Caine could not stand the sight of so many riders heading straight at him. For the first time in his life he was facing something he did not understand. Something which was testing his manhood and finding it wanting.

Hogan and Bearcutt watched in shock as Caine dragged his reins to one side and spurred his mount. They could hear the pathetic screams of their terrified confederate as he rode back in the direction of their town.

'Reckon there's just you and me now, Arthur.'

'Yep.' Bearcutt rested his rifle across his middle and watched as the dozen horsemen came ever closer.

17

Cole Brody pulled his reins back toward his chest and began to slow his lathered-up mount as he spotted the pair of horsemen illuminated by the large bright moon. He raised an arm and signalled his gang to meet his pace. Like a well-oiled machine, the eleven riders did as instructed.

Down to a mere canter, Cole Brody led his men towards the two defiant riders with a caution born out of countless similar episodes. His was a life which had cared little for the plight of others and it showed in his hooded eyes. As his mount trotted forward he pushed his coat over his gun and flicked off the leather safety-loop holding down its gleaming hammer.

'Looks like we got us a reception committee, boys,' Brody said loud enough for all of his men to hear clearly.

'You recognize the critters, Cole?' one of his men questioned as they rode straight at the two men.

Cole Brody squinted through the moonlight at the pair.

'I ain't seen them before. They ain't sporting badges though, so they can't be the law.'

'They could be hired guns,' Jones quipped as the line of twelve mounts slowed to a mere walk.

Cole Brody eased his reins back with his left hand until his horse stopped. His gang all followed suit.

'Could be gunfighters, Jones. Or just real stupid bastards.'

The cunning outlaw leader had seen the rifle in Bearcutt's lap and the glinting of Judge Hogan's pistol-barrel when they had been fifty yards apart. They were now a little over twenty feet away from the two riders.

'What's your business?' Judge Hogan asked in a voice that concealed his terror.

'Howdy. My name's Cole Brody.'

Hogan and Bearcutt might have lived in one of the remotest towns in the West but they had heard tell of the name which dripped proudly from the large man's lips.

'I'm Judge Hogan, Brody. State your business.'

Cole Brody leaned his large frame back against the cantle of his saddle as he stared hard at the two men. He found it difficult to fathom anyone who willingly risked their lives in such a cavalier fashion.

'You ain't hired guns?' Brody said in a surprised tone.

'Nope. We ain't hired guns, Brody,' Arthur Bearcutt snapped back quickly.

'What you want in Pueblo Flats?' Hogan repeated.

'Me and my boys are just visiting, Judge.' Brody sighed as he flexed the fingers of his right hand just above the pearl-handled grip of his holstered gun.

'We don't cotton to visitors, mister,' Bearcutt informed them.

'I said my name's Cole Brody. You heard of me?'

'We've heard of you, Brody,' Bearcutt announced as his fingers wrapped around the barrel of his rifle. 'Your sort ain't welcome in these parts.'

Brody glanced at his men to either side of him before smiling and returning his attention to the two brave souls facing them.

'We ain't looking for no trouble. Just a place to water our horses and buy provisions.'

'We ain't got no provisions to sell to your kind,' Bearcutt said firmly.

Judge Hogan pointed to where the river ran towards the very edge of the canyons.

'There's plenty of water there. Ain't no need for you and your gang to enter Pueblo Flats.'

'But we want to enter Pueblo Flats, Judge.' Brody grinned at the two riders.

'Turn your damn horses around and go back to where you come from. You ain't welcome in Pueblo Flats.' Hogan was beginning to feel more and more confident now that he had the measure of the stout outlaw leader. Brody looked nothing like men of his profession were meant to look, he thought. Brody had to weigh at least 250 pounds. Far too heavy for a gunman.

Brody started to laugh.

'You boys have spunk, and that's a fact.'

'We gonna let these storekeepers tell us what to do, Cole?' Jones asked as he sat watching the defiant riders before them.

Cole Brody slid his index finger over his trigger and then closed his grip around the handle of his weapon.

'Nope. We ain't gonna let these chicken-pluckers tell us where we can and can't go, Jones.'

There was a silence which seemed to last an eternity. Then the two riders from the small town saw the large man drawing his pistol, with a speed that defied reason. Hogan's eyes flashed from the gun in Brody's hand, along the line of outlaws. It was as if each and every one of them had somehow received a silent order to draw their own guns.

They obeyed the silent command with a speed that seemed to be totally unbelievable.

The bright moon danced off the barrels of the twelve guns which had suddenly cleared their holsters.

Judge Bevis Hogan let out a yell as he frantically raised his own gun and tried vainly to match Brody's speed. It was a brave but utterly pointless exercise.

Arthur Bearcutt had spotted the flashing gun-metal seconds before his companion. He lifted and aimed his rifle as quickly as he was able. He had hunted long before his whiskers had turned grey but this was different. This time his prey was able and willing to fire back.

Blinding venom spewed in both directions from the barrels of the drawn arsenal as deafening explosions matched every squeeze of the triggers.

A cloud of black gunsmoke hung heavily on the cool night air as bullets sped back and forth across the distance between the two groups of riders.

A chilling scream cut through the noise of the guns.

Judge Bevis Hogan was lifted inches above his saddle by the combined impact of a half-dozen bullets tearing through his flesh.

Blood seemed to spurt from every one of his deadly wounds as death claimed him.

Before Judge Hogan's bullet-riddled body had rolled off the back of his startled mount, Arthur Bearcutt had managed to pull his rifle trigger once more before he too was impacted by the deadly lead.

It was a good shot. A shot worthy of Bearcutt's once skilful past. An outlaw named simply Deuce felt the rifle bullet tearing through his chest and bursting his heart. It would be the last thing Deuce would ever feel. As he rolled off his horse and hit the ground, Cole

Brody had emptied his remaining shells into Bearcutt, causing the man's horse to buck violently.

The eleven remaining outlaws watched through the haze of gunsmoke as the terrified mount beneath Bearcutt's life-less body bolted off across the flat sand towards the rim of the mysterious canyons. Arthur Bearcutt had not fallen from his saddle before the fleeing horse rode straight off the edge of a cliff and fell into the dark abyss.

There was a silence amongst the outlaws as they checked themselves for wounds. They found none.

Cole Brody emptied his spent shells from his gun before hastily reloading it. It was a habit he had learned long ago and one which had saved his life more times than he could remember with any accuracy. A loaded pistol was a weapon, whilst an empty one was just an expensive hammer.

Lance Parker gazed down at the body of Deuce and then nudged his horse closer to Brody. There was a look in his eyes that even the moonlight could not disguise.

It was pure fear.

'I still don't cotton to this, Cole. Deuce was a good gun and he's now buzzard bait,' Parker muttered.

'We don't need him,' Brody said confidently as he holstered the six-shooter.

'We've lost four men in the last couple of months, Cole. We can't keep losing gunhands like this.' Parker was weary of the life they had all somehow found themselves trapped in. There seemed an inevitability about each of their own fates.

'Pueblo Flats is about ten miles or so in that direction, Lance.' Cole Brody pointed into the distance where faint lights could just be made out in the darkness. 'I reckon we just killed their entire defence. All we gotta do is ride on in and get what we came here for.'

Jones rode his horse straight up to the two riders facing one another.

'They must have women in that

town, boys. Ripe women just ready for the plucking. I want me a fat sassy female.'

Cole Brody's face was smiling again.

'Jones is right. That's all you and the rest of the boys need, Lance. A couple of good women to service. When was the last time you sowed some oats, boy?'

'I had me some fun back in Ravens Creek,' Parker lied.

'You ain't dropped them britches in over a year, boy.' Brody laughed, turning his reins.

Before Parker could say another word, the other riders had spurred their mounts and started heading towards the lights which attracted them like moths to a flame.

He shook his head and gave the bodies a last look before urging his horse to follow the other outlaws. Maybe Cole Brody was right. The wily old outlaw had lived a long time by being right more times than being wrong, after all.

Maybe it was true and all he needed to calm down his shattered nerves was to climb between the open thighs of a female.

Lance Parker caught up with the rest of the gang and nodded at the still smiling face of Brody. The leader of the outlaws touched the brim of his Stetson in reply.

The eleven riders continued on towards their target. There were more men to kill, gold to steal and women to pleasure among the alluring lights of Pueblo Flats.

18

The ominous echoes of the brief but deadly gun-battle were still bouncing off the walls of the lush canyon oasis as the startled mustang-men cautiously edged towards the broken bodies of Arthur Bearcutt and his hapless mount. They lay at the foot of the massive sand rockface with only the flickering flames of the wranglers' camp-fire and the shafts of moonlight illuminating their destruction. They had fallen out of the sky above the five men's heads and landed beside the tranquil lake.

What had seemed like paradise only a few minutes earlier, was now yet another gallery to the macabre brutality of the outside world. The five mustang-hunters had suddenly become aware that they were not alone in this strange remote place. There were others high above them. By the look of the dead rider, they were killers. Cold-blooded killers. The corpse was a gruesome sight, even for the hardened mustang-men.

Tan Gibson waded through the mud until he was standing next to the awesome vision. He had witnessed most things in his long eventful life but this had shocked him. His eyes surveyed the carnage and it chilled him to see the bullet-riddled body with his boots still in the stirrups of his saddle. Whoever this unlucky rider had once been, it was obvious that he had been dead before the crazed horse ran off the clifftop, Gibson mused.

'What in tarnation is going on here, Tan?' Fred Scott asked as he too moved cautiously to the side of his young friend and was able to get a closer look at the horrific sight.

Gibson felt his blood run cold as he stared upward to where the horse had fallen from. It was quiet up there now, he thought, but only minutes earlier there had been a battle being waged.

He wondered who this dead rider had been fighting, and why.

'I ain't got no idea what's going on, Fred. But something up there sure was none too healthy for this varmint.'

'Maybe it was just an old-fashioned showdown and this unlucky critter was the loser.' Keno Smith offered a helping hand to the pair of men as they stepped back on to solid ground once again.

'You could be right, Keno.' Tan Gibson nodded as he walked away from the brutal scene and on towards the line of tethered horses.

'Where you going in such a hurry?' Rufas Blake asked as the tall wrangler reached the horses and began inspecting his refreshed pinto.

Tan Gibson glanced at the faces of his men before picking up his horse blanket off the ground and throwing it over the back of his quiet mount.

'I've always had this curious streak in my nature. When something like this happens, I just got to find out why.'

Fred Scott moved through the other

men and squared up to Gibson, who was lifting his saddle off the ground.

'You ain't thinking of riding up there to take yourself a look, are you?'

'Yep. That's what I'm thinking all right, old timer,' Tan Gibson said as he lifted the stirrup and hooked it over the saddle horn.

'Don't be so darn stupid, Tan,' Scott implored.

Tan Gibson reached beneath the belly of his pinto and pulled one of the cinch straps up until it slid through the metal fastening. He then repeated the action with the second cinch strap. Gibson was silent as he worked on his Texan saddle. A saddle designed for men of his demanding nature.

'So you reckon I'm crazy, old man?'

'Crazy and loco!' Scott added.

Gibson paused and grinned.

'Hell, Fred, you gotta be plumb loco to be a mustang man, ain't you? No sane critter would risk their neck the way we do to earn a living.'

'Quit smiling when I'm talking to

you, boy.' Scott tried to use his fatherly image to dissuade Tan Gibson from doing something which might just prove fatal.

'I'm going up there to take me a look, Fred. That's just the way it is. I've got to find out what's going on and why somebody's killing folks.'

'But it ain't none of your business. We are here to catch us a mess of mustangs. Nothing else.' Scott sighed heavily.

Rufas Blake cleared his throat and walked up to the man whom he trusted with his life. A man he had learned to follow.

'You want some company?'

'Sure, Rufas. I'd be honoured to have your company on this little ride.' Gibson patted the man on his arm and watched as he immediately turned to the stack of saddles and plucked one off the ground. He had chosen Sol Kane's saddle and walked towards the unfortunate wrangler's horse.

'You figure young Sol would mind

if'n I use his gear and his gelding, Tan?' Rufas asked thoughtfully.

'Young Sol would be proud to have you use his goods, Rufas.' Tarp Gibson nodded at the quiet man.

'You figuring on going gallivanting without me, Tan?' Rainbow asked as he stepped towards the saddles and found the one which had belonged to their dead pal, Joe Green.

'You hankering for a little ride in the moonlight too?' Tan Gibson smiled as he watched Rainbow laying a blanket over the back of Joe Green's horse.

Rainbow manoeuvred his saddle on to the back of the horse.

'Sounds a tad too romantic to miss, Tan.'

'That's right, Rainbow. There could be a whole herd of gun-toting females up there just waiting to greet us.' Gibson chuckled.

Keno Smith said nothing as he found his own saddle and carried it towards his horse. Without uttering a single word he prepared his mount with a speed and precision common to men in his profession.

'You coming along too, Keno?' Tan Gibson asked as he watched the wrangler tightening his cinch straps on his own mount with expert hands.

'You might run into trouble without me along, Tan. If'n you do, you'll need someone who can hit what they shoot at,' Keno replied.

'Are you really that good with a gun, Keno?' Gibson asked with a wry smile.

'You better believe it. Ain't no better shot this side of the Pecos River, Tan,' came the reply.

'Somehow I figured that.' Gibson glanced at Rainbow and Rufas Blake who were leading their saddled mounts away from the line of wagon-horses. 'If one of us has to be good with a gun, it has to be Keno Smith.'

'Damn right!' Smith managed a grin before holding on to his saddle horn and mounting the tall buckskin.

'You other boys better make sure your guns are loaded,' Gibson said to

Blake and Rainbow. 'We don't want to let Keno do all the shooting up there, if there's any trouble.'

'Are all you boys losing your minds?' Fred Scott ranted helplessly.

Gibson rested a hand on Fred Scott's shoulder and stared hard into the old man's eyes. 'You stay here and fix us up a mess of biscuits, Fred. I don't figure this will take long.'

Scott shook his head.

'You keep your nose out of any trouble up there, boy. I'm too damn old to train a new boss.'

Gibson hopped into his stirrup and threw his right leg over the pinto. Turning the horse around whilst he waited for his men to mount their own horses, he winked down at Scott.

'I love you too, old-timer. Now get making them biscuits.'

Fred Scott watched as the tall rider atop the pinto led the way towards the steep incline. The four expert horsemen began to navigate the narrow trail in single file.

The moonlight danced on their shoulders as they slowly headed up towards the desolate prairie. Each rider was well aware that they were more than likely heading into the very jaws of death itself, but they were unable to ignore the possibility that someone might need their help.

Fred Scott knew he should have stopped them, but was wise enough to know also that men such as Gibson and the rest of their outfit were not easily dissuaded from doing what they believed was right.

It was not easy to distract mustang men from showing their sheer bravery. In fact it was probably impossible.

19

The horrendous sound of the devastatingly brief but effective battle had reached the ears of the surprised residents of Pueblo Flats long before the terrified Marvin Caine's horse rode back into their small town.

Caine had been at full gallop when the shooting had started behind his sweat-soaked spine. Yet he had neither looked back or even considered returning to help his friends. He had driven his spurs deep into the flesh of his mount and ridden on and on towards the lights of his town. If ever the term 'fair-weather friend' had been applied to any man, it applied to him.

Men stood like statues beside their chattering spouses unable to comprehend what was going on out there in the darkness. The sound of the vicious gunfire had drawn every one of the citizens of the tiny community from their homes. Jacob Fuller had strolled from his adobe home still carrying the Bible he had been reading. Seeing Caine driving his horse towards them made the elderly man begin to wonder what fate had befallen his cousin, Bevis Hogan.

Fuller had long been the righteous conscience of Pueblo Flats but it had been many years since any of the townspeople had given him a second thought. For they had long considered themselves as being superior to all less fortunate creatures and in no need of spiritual guidance.

Caine had reached the mass of people and dismounted before they seemed able to understand that he alone would be returning to their fold. Only Jacob Fuller seemed capable of understanding that this sweating, wide-eyed rider had something to hide. To Fuller, it was written in every bead of sweat trickling down the face of Caine. The Bible-clutching man knew guilt when he saw it, and he saw it clearly, even in the lantern-light.

'Where's Bevis?' Fuller's voice boomed.

The question was ignored by Caine as he wrapped his reins around a hitching pole and glanced back at the dark plain behind him.

'Where's Bearcutt and the judge?' a score of voices seemed to ask in unison as the sweating Caine staggered into the saloon and began searching for his courage in a whisky bottle at the long wooden bar.

'What was all that shooting?'

'Who was shooting?'

'Where are Bevis and Arthur?'

Marvin Caine had managed to swallow a third of the bottle before he was able to answer:

'Riders! A dozen riders! They came out of nowhere!'

'What do you mean?' a woman shouted at the blinking Caine as he leaned against the long bars shaking from head to toe.

'They must be a gang of outlaws.

They just started shooting at us and I managed to escape.' Caine took another mouthful of the strong liquid and swallowed. It did not seem to help him manage to look anyone in the eyes.

'You mean that the judge and old Arthur are dead?' another female from the crowd around him asked angrily.

'I'm not sure. It all happened so fast. The riders just started shooting without a warning. I shot back at them but they were like demons or something. They just kept on coming. We all turned our horses and started riding back here and that's the last I seen of the judge and Arthur.'

'You're a very brave man, Marve,' yet another woman said as the people gathered around the drinking Caine.

'Maybe old Bevis and Arthur are still riding for home,' a man offered from behind a huge woman. 'They might just not be as good a horseman as Marve.'

Marvin Caine felt his chest swelling with the unexpected and undeserved praise that was aimed at him. For a brief moment the cowardly wretch seemed to be wallowing in the waters that heroes often frequent.

It was ended a few seconds later.

'You didn't just leave them there to fight them riders alone, did you?' The voice of a man this time cut through the crowd. It was Jacob Fuller.

Caine looked up as Fuller stood directly before him. Even age could not diminish the power in the one-time preacher's voice.

'What?'

Fuller reached down to Caine's gunbelt and lifted the holster away from the sweating man's thigh. The truth was there for all to see.

'You say that you fired at the riders?'

'Yep. I did, Jacob. Why?' Caine replied in a faltering tone that seemed to bring the crowd closer.

'Then how come the safety loop is still holding down the gun-hammer, Marve?' Fuller growled.

'What?' Caine looked down at the holster in Fuller's hand. He watched as the older man flicked the small leather loop off the gun-hammer, removed the pistol from its holster and raised it to his nose.

'This gun ain't been fired, you lying toad,' Fuller said as he opened the chamber and stared at the bullets. 'None of these bullets have been used. You never fired one shot. You just hightailed it out of there like the coward you are, Marve.'

Caine began to move away from the hostile crowd.

'It ain't the way it looks, Jacob.'

Fuller raised the Bible until it was beneath the nose of the shaking man.

'Will you swear on this that you're telling the truth, boy?' Marvin Caine's eyes flashed around the angry faces of the gathered crowd. Faces which, unlike that of Jacob Fuller, were not the sort to forgive.

'I . . . I was scared. Them riders just opened up on us. I didn't have a chance to do nothing.'

'Except leave your friends to face a

dozen riders on their own,' Fuller spat.

'It ain't like that. We was ambushed,' Caine screamed back at the stern-featured old man who was bearing down on him with all the other irate citizens of Pueblo Flats at his side.

'You yellow bastard!' someone yelled.

'You coward!' another added.

'You rat!'

'The snivelling wretch!'

'How could you desert them?'

'We ought to string him up!'

'Hanging's too good for him!'

Marvin Caine suddenly realized he might have escaped the twelve riders but was now facing a much larger crowd of angry people. People who had in the past strung up those who had betrayed them.

'The riders!' a voice from outside the saloon called. 'They're here!'

As Caine blinked hard, desperately trying to make the effects of the whisky disappear, the entire crowd rushed out into the dark street.

Moving across the saloon towards the

open doors, he heard the sound of approaching hoofs. A sudden chill raced up his yellow spine.

Cole Brody and his remaining ten riders were thundering towards the remote town at a pace which would bring them into the array of buildings within a few minutes.

20

Darkness offered no protection to Pueblo Flats. The brilliant moon told the ruthless riders exactly where it lay clearly enough but it was the flickering street-lanterns that seemed to shine out across the flat landscape like beacons attracting them like flies to a dung heap. Cole Brody could hardly believe his eyes at the sight before them. The town was nothing more than a series of adobe structures. Hardly better to look at than the poorest Mexican buildings south of the Texas border. It seemed impossible for Brody to comprehend that this insignificant-looking town could be harbouring a fortune in gold dust, yet that was the lure which had brought him and his gang here.

Reining in a mere hundred yards from the livery-stable corral, Brody brought his men to a halt. For a moment he had no idea why he had stopped his horse, but as he sat in his saddle amongst his outlaws, he realized what was eating at him.

As Brody had come within sight of the well illuminated town he had seen scores of men, women and children rushing around in the streets. Sixty years of experience had taught him the value of caution.

Holding on to his reins as tightly as he could, Brody called across to Jones, who rode his horse up beside his own.

'Look at the place, Jones.'

'Sure seems a tad busy, Cole.'

'Most small towns like this tend to go to sleep when the sun goes down, don't they?' Brody thought aloud.

'Maybe our shots woke the critters up.'

That was it. That was what had caused him to stop his horse in mid-flight. Pueblo Flats was alive with wide-awake folks rushing in and out of their homes. Their brief encounter eight miles back and the gunbattle it produced must have echoed around this flat range and sent the entire population into a frenzied panic.

'This ain't the way we planned it, is it?' Jones asked his troubled leader.

'Nope. This ain't the way we thought it would be, Jones,' Brody replied as he glanced along the ranks of his riders. This was going to be harder than he had first thought. He always liked to ride into a town when most of its people were either asleep or just plain drunk. There were women and even children running around in the light of the large moon and the glowing street-lanterns. He had lost the element of surprise and it might prove costly.

'We must have woken the critters up when we gunned down them two old men, Cole,' Lance Parker cried across the neck of his agitated mount.

'I knew those two old men were trouble,' Cole Brody snarled as he tried to soothe his eager horse. 'Shooting them has brought every damn one of the townspeople out of the woodwork. Damn!'

Jones eyed the milling crowd.

'They don't look as if they could make much of a fight of it, Cole.'

'Maybe not.'

'They might try and make a fight of it,' the brooding Parker said grimly.

'Quit talking, Lance. I'm starting to get sick of the sound of your belly aching,' Brody said whilst watching the crowd with caution.

'Do you see any guns?'

'Nope, but that don't mean there ain't any.'

'What we gonna do, Cole?' a voice asked the hooded-eyed outlaw.

'We will do exactly what we came here to do,' Brody responded quickly.

'I don't like the idea of killing women and children, Cole,' Jones said honestly.

'It won't be the first time.'

There was a deafening silence along the line of outlaws as they steadied their horses. Each one of them knew that it was true. Each had killed their fair share of women and children over the years for one reason or another. Yet hearing it from the lips of Cole Brody seemed to unsettle them. He knew exactly how to make them come to heel. How to pull their strings like the puppet master he was.

They had to obey. There was no alternative. For only one man had ever controlled this gang. There had never been any pretenders to his throne.

Cole Brody drew his Winchester from beneath his saddle and cocked its well-oiled mechanism. With gritted teeth he nodded to the riders on his left and then those to his right.

Once again, it was as if a silent order had been passed to them by their infamous leader. They all pulled their long rifles from their scabbards and readied them.

'Let's kill us some pilgrims, boys.'

The eleven riders kicked back their spurs and unleashed their fury. The horses thundered across the hundred yards between themselves and the town. With every stride their horses took, they fired.

The chilling screams of terrified people filled the air, but it did not stop the eleven outlaws from coming. They could smell the gold dust in their nostrils. Taste the wealth that this town had hidden from the outside world for so many years. Nothing could stop the thundering riders.

Some of the men and women of Pueblo Flats had found enough time to locate weapons. Some had even managed to fire them at the yelling riders who tore into their town.

Yet most were just trying to find a place to hide. A place which did not exist.

There were no hiding-places for the innocent in Pueblo Flats this night. Only death might spare them from what would come later when Brody unleashed his men and permitted their unholy vices to spill over on to the survivors.

Cole Brody had not lived for six

decades without learning a few tricks about survival, and he displayed them all as he led his riders through the streets of Pueblo Flats, shooting at everyone who got in his way.

His fourteen-shot repeating rifle spewed out lead with such venom, even his own followers found it hard to believe. Brody seemed unable to miss with the longbarrelled rifle. Those he did not shoot, he simply rode down with his horse.

Men, women and children fell to his bullets or beneath the hoofs of his charging mount. The few people who had weaponry tried vainly to shoot the leader of the outlaw pack. Yet still no bullet seemed able to find his ample frame as he led his ten followers through the wide moonlit streets. Once again, Cole Brody seemed to defy death itself.

It was a point not missed by those who rode behind him. Brody seemed invincible.

The feeble attempt from the few

townspeople who had managed to get their hands on rifles and guns made little impact on the riders as they rode after their leader into the heart of the small community. Two of the outlaws were hit by wild shots from the panic-stricken guns of the Pueblo Flats people. It was too little, too late.

Jones expertly killed everyone he spotted holding anything resembling a weapon. It seemed that only the women had found the desired courage required to fight, and it was they who had paid the greatest price. But for every female they gunned down, there seemed to be two more rushing around the streets.

This was no normal raid conducted by normal men. This was carnage. Yet the riders were no strangers to such acts of horrific violence. This was not the first town they had ridden into with their weapons blazing.

Blood covered the streets of the tiny town before the nine remaining outlaws surrounded what was left of the stunned community. Even in the moonlight it was obvious that the streets had turned scarlet with the slaughter.

Cole Brody sat on his horse, quickly loading his Winchester once again, and watched his men herd the surviving townspeople into the middle of the wide street.

'How many of them are left?' Brody called out, not looking up from his rifle as he slid bullets into its breech.

'About fifty,' Parker replied.

'How many men?'

'Fifteen or so.'

Brody rode up to the riders and stared down at the bemused faces of their captives.

'Kill the men.'

A wailing erupted from within the heart of their prisoners as the females and children suddenly realized that the stout elderly rider with the heavily lidded eyes was going to kill what was left of their menfolk.

Brody seemed to care little as he leaned closer to Jones.

'Cut out the women and children. Take them to the bank until we need them.'

'There's a heap of kids in this bunch, Cole.' Lance Parker pointed down at the whimpering crowd.

Brody glanced up and smiled.

'Keep the girls. I know how much some of you hombres *hanker* after girls.'

'And the boys?'

'Kill the little brats.'

'Where should we do it? Here?'

'Nope. Not here. There's too many corpses here already.' Brody looked up and stared around the array of simple structures.

'Then where?' Jones seemed eager to get on with the job, and it showed.

'Take the pathetic bastards downwind to the livery stable and then shoot them. Then search every one of these houses. There might just be a few strays hiding under the beds.' Brody was smiling as he aimed his horse toward the well-lit saloon. He was thirsty.

21

The four mustang men had only just reached the top of the narrow trail which led up from the deep canyon and were allowing their horses to get their second wind when they heard the hideous sound of gun-play dancing on the warm air all around them. It was like the haunting music of death.

At first none of the quartet could quite make out where the brutal battle was taking place. Each of the dust-caked riders stared out into the darkness which surrounded them, trying to figure it out. It was then that Tan Gibson noticed the wild birds flying in the moonlit sky above their heads. Tapping Rainbow on the shoulder he pointed heavenward.

'I seen birds before. What's your point?' Rainbow shrugged.

'Them birds ain't flying at this time

of night because they want to,' Gibson noted.

'Sure! They're putting distance between themselves and whoever it is doing the shooting,' Rainbow said, looking in the direction that the birds had come from.

'Which means we ought to head thataway.' Gibson aimed his finger over Rainbow's shoulder. Neither man knew it but that was where Pueblo Flats was situated. None of the four had any idea it even existed.

Keno Smith looped his reins over the head of his mount and stepped into his stirrup before hauling himself into his saddle.

'By the sound of it, there's a war going on.'

'A war or a massacre, Keno,' Gibson said drily as he held on to the mane of his pinto.

Rufas Blake rubbed his knees before he, too, mounted. His face showed signs of the worry he was secretly harbouring.

'You OK, Rufas?' Gibson asked as he threw himself on to the back of his pinto.

'Don't fret about me. It sounds like there are others in real need of help out there someplace.'

'No aches and pains?' Keno raised a surprised eyebrow in Blake's direction.

'Nope. I'm just scared,' Rufas Blake admitted as he steadied his mount.

'Me too,' Keno agreed.

Gibson stood in his saddle and screwed up his eyes as he surveyed the land before them. Everything seemed blue as the moon bathed over the entire landscape. For the first time in his life, Gibson realized his eyesight was not what it once had been.

'Can anyone see what's out there?' Gibson asked, holding his reins tightly in his gloved hands.

Rainbow raised a flat hand above his eyebrows and squinted out at the parched land before them. The sound of gunfire was still echoing as he lowered his arm again.

'I see lights, Tan. Reckon they must be street-lanterns or the like.'

'Yeah?' Gibson stared hard again at the distant blur which was the horizon. He still could not see them.

'I can see them too, Tan,' Keno chipped in as he allowed his horse to walk to the side of the pinto.

'Damned if I can see them,' Gibson frowned.

'Old age, Tan. It comes to us all if'n we don't die first,' Rufas Blake said as he tried to comfort the older wrangler.

'Hush up,' Gibson told Blake before looking at Rainbow who was still studying the horizon. 'Are you sure you can see lights or are you just joshing?'

'I ain't joshing, Tan. They must be about nine miles away,' Rainbow added as he wrapped his reins around his left hand and started his mount moving.

Rufas tapped his spurs and began to allow his horse to ride towards the place where all hell had broken loose a handful of minutes earlier. Gibson and Keno spurred their mounts and soon drew level with their friends.

'You hear that?' Tan Gibson said to Rainbow as the horses all began to make pace.

There was a sound hanging on the prairie air which was in total contrast to the gunfire.

'I hear something, but I'm damned if I know what it is,' Rainbow said as he felt his horse gathering pace with every heartbeat.

Drawing closer and closer to the faint lights which were Pueblo Flats, the four mustang men felt the animals beneath their Texas saddles quickening. The four riders were now standing in their stirrups, taking the weight off their horses' backs and allowing the highly trained creatures to gallop. The experienced horses did not require whipping or the thrust of razor-sharp spurs to encourage them. These were thoroughbred cutting horses belonging to the mustang men and they would ride until their hearts burst if commanded.

Stride after stride the long-limbed

mounts ate up the bone-dry ground beneath their hoofs.

Tan Gibson gripped his reins in one hand, and held the saddle horn in the other as his pinto matched the other horses for speed. Now he could see the glowing of the distant street-lanterns as their amber light twinkled across the distance between them.

Whatever was happening in Pueblo Flats was bloody. The four riders had heard too many shots for it to be anything else. The sound of bullets as they exploded from the lethal barrels of rifles and pistols ahead of them, filled their ears and chilled their minds.

What were they riding into? Gibson kept asking himself as he slowly edged his pinto ahead of the three other mounts. Why were they sticking their noses into somebody else's business? Gibson knew the answer, it was the only way people like them could sleep at night.

Then they heard the strange noise once more.

This time they knew what it was.

It was the sound of a solitary church bell ringing out. For a moment it was like listening to the wailing of a heart-broken angel pleading for someone to help. Its pleas would not go unanswered.

As each of the four riders recognized the sound as being that of a bell, they glanced across at one another. The expression on their faces denoted confusion.

Total confusion.

What on earth was the sound of a church bell doing amid the blasts of rifles and pistols?

Thundering on and on towards their goal, the mustang men began to wonder again what they were heading towards. What horrors awaited them when they reached the lights of the town? Could they, mere mustang men, possibly be of any assistance to whoever it was on the receiving end of all those bullets?

Yet, even racked by self-doubt, none

of the four expert horsemen allowed their pace to slow for even a single stride. They continued driving their mounts towards those strangely haunting lanterns which flickered their light over the level range.

Tan Gibson felt his pinto suddenly loosen up beneath him and find a flowing stride which drew him further ahead of his three companions.

He allowed the pinto to continue forging away from the other horses. Gibson knew this horse well and realized it would be pointless wasting energy trying to hold it in check. If nothing else, Gibson would be first to arrive at the town of adobes which he could now see.

First to face whatever or whoever it was discharging all that lethal lead.

First to be challenged and probably first to face death itself. Yet he was unafraid. Death had never held any fear for the man who had broken so many bones as a mustang man. Gibson's only fear was of the unknown.

What lay out there in the flickering lantern-light was a mystery to the brave riders.

Then the sound of the ringing church bell filled his ears once again. Tan Gibson felt a chill running along his spine. It was not the night air that caused him to shudder.

It was something else.

Now his nostrils could smell the acrid stench of gunpowder as he drew even closer to Pueblo Flats.

Tan Gibson narrowed his eyes and thundered on.

22

Cole Brody had moved away from the long bar with the thimble glass in one hand and the bottle of expensive whiskey in the other. He chewed on the end of the long black cigar as its smoke drifted into his half-closed eyes.

'Jones!'

The scream of Brody's voice seemed to stop the outlaws in their tracks. Each of them paused as they waited for their leader to call out again before continuing with their gruesome chores.

'Jones!' Brody yelled out again.

Jones ran across the wide expanse of street towards the saloon at a speed only managed by men who fear the consequences of incurring the wrath of vermin like Cole Brody.

Having managed to sidestep all the bodies, Jones crashed through the swing-doors of the well-lit saloon and entered. When he saw the face of Brody, the outlaw skidded to a halt.

'What's wrong, Cole?'

'Listen you half-wit. Listen,' Brody said as he rested the bottle on a round card-table and then plucked the cigar from his thin lips.

Jones nervously edged to the side of the stout man and did as he was commanded. He listened.

At first he heard nothing but the shots coming from down at the livery stable. Shots which were dispatching the male citizens of Pueblo Flats to their maker.

Then Jones suddenly realized what Cole Brody meant. The ringing of a church bell resounded all around the blood-soaked buildings.

'You hear it?' Brody asked through a plume of smoke.

'Yep. It's a bell.' Jones stepped to the swing-doors and peered out over the top of them.

'It ain't just a bell. I reckon it's a church bell, Jones. Somewhere out there we got ourselves a varmint ringing a church bell,' Brody said.

'I ain't seen no church. Have you?' Jones asked blankly, trying to locate the source of his leader's irritation. None of the buildings in Pueblo Flats looked remotely like any sort of church he had ever seen.

'One of these adobes must double as some kind of church, Jones. Get a few of the boys together and find out which one.' Cole Brody washed the whiskey down his fat throat and then poured himself another.

'And the bellringer?' Jones hesitated as he waited for his instructions. 'Shall I kill him?'

Cole Brody sucked on the thick smoke of his cigar.

'Nope. Don't kill the stupid critter. Just catch him and then bring the bastard to me. I'll teach him some old-time religion, Jones.'

'Amen to that.' Jones rushed out into the street and whistled at two of the outlaws who were idle. The pair followed him without question for they had seen him coming from the saloon. They had also seen the unmistakable figure of Brody standing just inside the swing-doors of the drinking-hole, giving Jones his orders.

It did not pay to upset Cole Brody. Not when he had the taste of death in his mouth. A flavour he savoured above all others.

★   ★   ★

'Stop the train!' Marshal Vincent demanded. Both he and his deputy had spotted Pueblo Flats across the rim of the jagged canyon as the locomotive sped down the steep gradient. They could see their ultimate destination and also hear the blood-curdling sound of gunshots. The lawmen knew that Cole Brody and his gang had not only arrived at the small, seemingly insignificant, town but had started killing its occupants.

'I said stop this damn train!' Vincent

shouted at the guard in the rear coach.

'We can't stop here, Marshal Vincent.' The guard shrugged trying not to allow his nerves to show whilst facing the two law officers.

'We have to stop here. Right now,' Ericson growled.

'Can't you boys wait until morning? The train has to stop for water down on the flats. You can get off then,' the guard said.

Vincent sighed heavily before drawing one of his pistols and ramming its barrel into the face of the man.

'Stop the train.'

The shaking guard slowly got to his feet and swallowed hard.

'Why here?'

'We have to get to Pueblo Flats as soon as possible. We ain't got no time to waste,' Ericson informed him.

'But there's a damn canyon between here and Pueblo Flats.' The guard raised his arm as his fingers searched for the emergency cord hanging above their heads. 'It's suicide to try and ride from here to that town. You'll have to ride across the very rim of that canyon. One false step by them horses of yours and you'll fall to your deaths.'

'Maybe we're better riders than you think, mister,' Ericson said forcefully.

'But that's an impossible ride in the daytime let alone at night, boys,' the guard gasped as he was forced towards the wall of the long coach-car.

'It's a risk we're willing to take.' Vincent screwed his eyes up and glared hard at the trembling shorter man.

'But . . . '

Vincent prodded the gun into the cheek of the railway guard.

'Pull it. Just pull the cord and stop this train.'

'You heard the marshal,' Ericson added.

'OK! I don't get paid enough to get gun-whipped.' The guard obeyed. The massive train began to screech to a reluctant halt, sending sparks floating into the air. Vincent holstered his gun and led his deputy out on to the platform of the coach. Leaping across on to the flat car, both lawmen moved to their horses and released the leg-hobble restraints from their mounts. They waited for the locomotive to come finally to a stop.

Before the engineer had walked half-way down the length of his massive train, he saw the two lawmen jumping down from the flat car atop their horses.

The sweating guard emerged from the interior of the coach-car and stared at the pair of horsemen as they disappeared down the steep slope towards the perilous rim of the canyon.

'Who in tarnation was that, Earl?' the engineer shouted at the guard as he approached.

'It was just a pair of loco lawmen in one hell of a hurry, Pete,' came the reply.

★　★　★

Jacob Fuller had not sought a gun or a rifle when the Brody gang had been spotted. He had lived far too long to panic at the sight of deadly riders even when they were unleashing their bullets into the very bodies of innocent men, women and children. Fuller had simply walked to his modest home and bolted the heavy door before moving out into the high-walled garden.

Having placed his beloved Bible on a table he proceeded to the one object he valued. Mounted on a solid wooden frame, which was rumoured to have once been a gallows, Fuller had stared at the large brass bell he had brought with him all the way from New England.

As the sound of gunfire grew louder and the screams more sickening, he prayed. When his prayers had been completed he held on to the long bell-cord and started to pull with all his strength.

He was ancient now and it had taken nearly ten minutes for his cord-wasted muscles to create enough momentum on the long cord for the bell to start ringing out. Why the old man, who had shunned the gold dust of his fellow townspeople, had decided to ring his cherished church bell, only he knew.

It might have seemed a stupid thing to do, to attract the attention of hardened killers to your existence and location by ringing a loud bell which could be heard for miles. If you were the sort who valued your own life above all other things, it could have been thought of as suicidal, yet Jacob Fuller had faith.

Even in the middle of a bloody massacre, he had faith. Total, uncompromising faith.

As he heard the sound of his bolted door being battered into a million splinters behind him, Fuller continued mustering every ounce of his dwindling powers and continued to pull the bell-cord.

Even when he heard the outlaws running towards his bowed spine and felt the cold steel of their gun-barrels, he somehow continued to make his bell ring out.

A hundred threats could not stop Fuller. With blood dripping from his old hands as the rough bell-cord slid through his determined grip, he carried on.

Only when Jones's gun was smashed down on the back of his skull, did he stop.

The three outlaws dragged the barely conscious Jacob Fuller from his secluded garden, through the house, out on to the street and back towards the saloon. He could hear the outlaws talking but could not understand a single word that spewed from their angry mouths. Fuller's eyes glared at the ground blankly as they carried him face down to their leader.

* * *

Cole Brody was standing a few paces inside the saloon when Jones and the two other outlaws threw their elderly prize on to the floor at his feet.

Brody looked down at the old man and began to laugh.

'This is our bellringing pal?'

'Yep, Cole. This is the varmint,' Jones nodded violently.

Jacob Fuller gazed around the floor. His eyes began to focus upon the spittoon just beside him. Its highly polished brass acted like a mirror. He could see each of the four men who were laughing at him. Without knowing why, he had drawn their deadly attention to himself and yet he did not regret having done so.

'You still alive, old man?' Brody shouted down through cigar smoke.

Fuller managed to turn his head and look at the boots of the outlaw leader. They were expensive boots purchased with the ill-gotten gains of murder and robbery.

'I'm not dead yet.'

Brody kicked Fuller hard enough to turn the man on to his back.

'Not yet, but soon.'

The chilling laughter filled the saloon.

'Then finish me off. I'm not scared of you or what you can or cannot do.' Fuller's words were powerfully spoken as he stared up at Brody.

The outlaw was impressed.

'You got nerve, old man. I've seen many a coward in my time but you ain't one.'

Jacob Fuller edged himself into a seated position with his back against the cold foot-rail that ringed the long wooden bar.

'Why don't you kill me? You seem to have killed everyone else in Pueblo Flats.'

Cole Brody reached down and grabbed the shirt-front of the old man and hauled him to his feet. There was a venom in the face of the outlaw. His hooded eyes searched the battered features for weakness, yet failed to find any.

'Why did you ring that damn bell, old

man?' Brody asked curiously.

'To muster help,' Fuller replied defiantly.

'Help? From where?' Brody laughed.

Jacob Fuller looked up briefly at the ceiling before returning his eyes to the stout man before him.

'The Lord!'

Jones started to laugh.

'Reckon he's a mite deaf, old-timer.'

Cole Brody glared hard into Fuller's eyes. He had seen this sort of courage before and it troubled him. He had learned to be wary of people who feared nothing except the wrath of their God.

'Is there gold in this town like the stories I've heard?'

Fuller nodded.

'More than you and your men could carry on your horses.'

Brody glanced at the faces of his three men before returning his attention to the man he held in his powerful grip.

'Where is it?'

'In the bank,' Fuller said freely.

Brody was puzzled.

'Is it in a vault?'

'No. It's in a large room behind the clerk's counter.'

'Who has the key?'

'It's not locked. Why should we lock it up? It belongs or belonged to all of us.' Fuller felt the strength returning to his legs as Brody's grip relaxed.

'You mean that you've a fortune in gold dust sitting in a room and the door ain't even locked?' Cole Brody released his grip in astonishment.

'There has never been any reason for us to lock the gold away. Why would any of us steal our own gold?' Jacob Fuller staggered back to the bar and rested his elbows upon the damp surface. He studied the men before him with the eye of a preacher. What he saw convinced him that there were still some souls it would be impossible to save.

Brody snapped his fingers at his men. 'Gather up what's left of the men,

Jones. We got us a bank to empty.'

Jacob Fuller hovered against the bar as the four men began to walk towards the swing-doors.

'Just one thing. Who are you, fat man?'

Cole Brody turned and drew a pistol. The shot seemed to hit the elderly man squarely. The outlaw leader had holstered his gun before Fuller's limp body hit the floor.

23

'Riders! I seen me some riders, Cole,' Lance Parker yelled, as he reached the swing-doors of the saloon and peered in over them.

'Riders? Where?' Cole Brody responded.

'I was with Casey finishing off them men and boys down at the livery, Cole. I seen them riding in.' Parker tried hard to catch his breath as he spoke.

Brody led the three other men out into the moonlight and stared to where Parker was indicating with a shaking finger.

'How many were there?'

'I spotted three before I come running to tell you,' Parker said. 'There could have been more. A lot more.'

Cole Brody leaned from the board-walk to his horse, pulled his Winchester from its scabbard beneath his saddle and cranked its mechanism.

'Round up the boys,' he ordered. 'Tell them we got visitors at the livery.'

Parker jumped off the boardwalk to the street and rushed off in the direction of the bank.

'How many of us are left?' Brody asked Jones in a hushed tone.

'Nine, as far as I can figure.' Jones shrugged.

'Ought to be enough.' Brody glanced at Jones who was standing just ahead of two of his least favourite outlaws. 'We'll take Vance and Harper with us. Lance will swing around from the bank with Casey and rest of the boys. We should be able to cut them riders down.'

Cole Brody began the long walk down the centre of the wide moonlit street towards the distant livery stable.

'Could be them damn marshals from Dodge, Jones,' Brody announced.

'They've been dogging our trail for too long, Cole,' Jones said as he pulled both his guns from their holsters and cocked their hammers.

'Damn right,' Brody sneered. 'Time we ended it.'

Tan Gibson had dismounted when he caught sight of the bodies lying in the large paddock next to the stables. He had seen two men running away as he had approached. He wondered if they were afraid or just out of ammunition. Neither possibility consoled him.

Rufas Blake, Rainbow and Keno arrived a minute or so after Gibson, and leapt from their horses with expert ease. When they reached the tall mustang-man, they too saw the horrific carnage which had stopped Gibson in his tracks.

'Oh God,' Blake said sadly.

Tan Gibson swallowed hard before looking at his three friends.

'I guess I've led you men into something you ain't gonna thank me for. If any of you want to head back to camp, I'll understand.'

'What are you gonna do, Tan?' Blake asked.

'I'm gonna try and find out who done this.'

'I'm with you,' Rainbow muttered, trying not to look at the limp bodies lying in a bloody pile. Even the soft blue light of the large moon could not sanitize the scene.

'You can count me in,' Keno said drawing his Colt and checking it carefully.

Rufas Blake walked back to his horse and pulled out his carbine from beneath the Texas saddle.

'We gotta find the bastards who done this and make them pay, Tan.'

'We ain't gunfighters, boys. We might be out of our depth.'

'We're all Texans, ain't we?' Keno Smith nodded.

'Damn right, Keno. We're Texans.' Gibson had hardly finished speaking when a volley of rifle shots rang out. The red-hot tapers sped over the four men's heads. They each dropped to the ground and stared hard into the murky gunsmoke which filled the long wide street. The moonlight seemed to blur everything except the flashes of the guns and rifles aimed in their direction. Round after round came from the weapons of Cole Brody and his gang.

Keno Smith crawled to the side of Gibson and pointed to their left where he had spotted several other figures moving towards them. Unknown to the mustang men it was Parker, Casey and the three remaining members of Brody's gang.

'We had better do something darn fast or we'll get caught up in a crossfire, Tan.'

Gibson bit his lower lip and screwed up his eyes.

'How many are there, Keno?'

'I see four men shooting and five more heading around over there,' Keno said, clutching his Colt close to his chest.

Gibson looked at Rainbow and Blake.

'Get the saddle ropes off the horses,' he shouted.

Rainbow and Rufas Blake crawled back to where their mounts were standing, removed the ropes from the saddle horns and then returned to the cover of the long fence-poles.

'We got the ropes. Now what do ya want us to do with them?' Rainbow called across the twenty-foot distance between them.

Tan Gibson's mind was racing. He was no gunfighter but he was an expert with a rope. He raised his hand slightly.

'Throw them to me, Rainbow.'

The wrangler tossed the coiled ropes to Gibson and then drew his own gun and checked it.

'What you gonna do, Tan?' Keno asked the brooding man at his side.

There was no reply. Tan Gibson could not answer the simple question. He stared hard at the ropes at his side.

Keno grabbed Gibson's arm and looked at the troubled face. He was about to repeat the question, when he realized Gibson was desperately trying to work out their next move.

Bullets skimmed over their heads again leaving the acrid aroma of burning air in their nostrils. The Brody gang were getting close. Too damn close.

'We gotta do something, Tan,' Keno said, raising his Colt.

Gibson looped one rope over his shoulder and held another in his gloved left hand.

'You said you were good with guns, Keno. Prove it and cover me.'

Keno had no time to reply. Gibson had leapt to his feet and darted across the ground to the line of horses. Grabbing the horn of his saddle, the mustang man swung up on to the back of his pinto and galloped hard across the flat level ground to their left.

With almost unbelievable ease, Gibson managed to make his pinto leap the three-bar fence poles. The horse landed in the livery stable corral and then galloped straight at the building.

Bullets blasted in from both sides of the fence poles as the outlaws tried frantically to shoot the thundering rider.

Keno Smith knelt, firing his Colt at the outlaws approaching from their left whilst Rainbow and Rufas Blake attempted to pick off the gunmen who were heading straight for them.

The night air was alive with flashing gun-blasts as deadly shells exploded from the array of weaponry.

Cole Brody had not faltered on his determined onslaught towards the strangers who had suddenly arrived in the town he had thought was well and truly beaten. Then as he had suddenly seen the rider jumping the livery fence poles, Brody felt the heat of bullets being returned in his direction.

Vance seemed to fall silently beside him as two Winchester shells ripped through his body. Then Harper cried out as he felt his right leg being smashed by bullets.

'The varmints have opened up on us, Cole,' Jones said before ducking behind the staggering Harper.

Brody turned around just in time to see Harper being hit again and falling heavily over the crouching figure of Jones. Without a single thought for his own safety, the outlaw leader cocked his Winchester and fired back at the distant mustang men.

Tan Gibson rode straight through the open large double doors of the livery stable. Dragging his reins up to his chest, Gibson turned his pinto around and quickly studied the interior of the large structure. Moonlight cascaded into the building from a half-dozen directions as the mustang man saw the hay loft above him.

Gibson slung a rope over a massive wooden joist above his head, stood on top of his saddle and then hauled himself up to the higher level.

He released the rope, moved to the open hay loft door and stared down on to the figures of Lance Parker and his four cohorts.

Swinging the rope in his skilled hands, Gibson lassoed three of the firing outlaws beneath him and dragged them off their feet before tying the rope around a wooden upright. Before he could look out of the high loft door, a score of bullets tore the wooden frame to shreds.

Tan Gibson rubbed the burning sawdust from his clothing, and ran towards the edge of the high loft. Whistling to his horse beneath him, Gibson was just about to leap down on to his saddle when a shot cut through his shirt.

Gibson reeled around in agony.

Falling backwards on to a pile of hay, Gibson gritted his teeth and checked his side. Blood poured from a deep gash. For a moment he just lay there listening to footsteps below him as more bullets blasted through the wooden parapet he was lying upon.

Gibson rolled away from the splintering wood and dragged his pistol from its holster. As he clambered to his knees he saw the two outlaws fanning their gunhammers up at him.

Without even aiming, the wounded mustang-man squeezed his trigger and sent the outlaw called Casey hurtling backwards into the stable wall. Then Gibson spotted Parker moving behind the skittish pinto.

With blood running down his side, Tan Gibson tried to take aim but could not see the outlaw clearly.

Then he remembered the other wrangler's rope coiled over his shoulder. Stepping back into the shadows, Tan Gibson unwound the rope and made a sixfoot-wide loop before he started to swing it carefully above his head. Faster and faster, Gibson twirled the rope until the loft was buzzing with the sound of the speeding fibre. With every movement of his right arm as he controlled the lasso, Gibson could feel blood weeping from his wound and running down his side.

Then he threw it.

Lance Parker heard the sound of the unwinding rope as it flew down from above him. For a moment, the outlaw could not tell where the expertly aimed lasso had gone. Ducking beneath the pinto, Parker stared like a frightened animal into the darkness of the livery stable loft.

To his surprise, the outlaw noticed the horse moving to its side away from him. Parker raised both his Remingtons and looked up at the side of the pinto. Then he saw the tight knot of the lasso wrapped around the saddle horn. Parker suddenly realized what Gibson had done. Roping the saddle horn had allowed the injured mustang-man to haul the pinto away from the hiding outlaw.

Lance Parker rose to his feet and fired both his pistols rapidly. The thick putrid gunsmoke blasted from both barrels as Parker moved to his right, hoping to get a better view of his target. As the two boots hit him squarely in his chest, Parker felt his ribs cave in. Gibson had looped the end of his long cutting-rope over the huge wooden joist and thrown himself off the high parapet. The pinto had moved because the saddle horn was taking the full weight of the wounded mustang-man as he was hurtling through the night air.

Gibson clambered to his feet slowly and looked at the two bodies before him. One was dead and the other not far off. Tan Gibson loosened the tight knot from his saddle horn and then dragged the long rope down from where it was hanging over the joist. Before he had time to do anything with the rope, Gibson's attention was drawn to the firing coming from outside the livery stable.

Drawing his pistol from his holster again, he cocked its blood-soaked hammer and staggered to the edge of the large open doorway. He could see the pair of gunmen to his left. They were still shooting at his three friends.

'Over here!' Gibson yelled at the two outlaws.

Cole Brody and Jones crawled under the bottom poles of the long fence and started firing in his direction. They were good, Gibson thought. Their bullets tore the edge of the large door apart and took his gun from his hand.

The tall mustang-man moved back into the livery and plucked his long rope off the ground. With desperate hands, he made a new lasso and started to rotate the rope over his head whilst watching the frame of the huge open door.

As the first figure's silhouette cautiously turned around the corner with both guns blazing, Gibson released the rope. He watched as the huge loop of the lasso floated through the night air and dropped over the man's shoulders. Hauling it with all his remaining strength, Gibson pulled Jones off his feet. As the outlaw's body hit the ground, one of Jones's pistols fired. The shot killed him instantly.

Tan Gibson backed off to where the two other outlaws lay and searched for one of their weapons in the darkness.

As he looked up, he saw the wide frame of Cole Brody entering the huge building. It was like looking into the face of death itself.

Now only shadows protected Gibson.

Brody had always lived a charmed existence. Even now, in the middle of a battle, no bullet had been able to claim his life nor come close to his ample frame. He stood in the doorway defying anyone to shoot him.

Tan Gibson stepped back until his back touched the wall and continued watching the deadly outlaw. Gibson wondered how long it would take for the man's eyes to adjust to the darkness and finally locate his wounded body with the Winchester in his hands.

The shooting seemed to stop and be replaced by the sound of riders. Tan Gibson recognized the voices of his yelling friends as they too leapt over the fence poles on their horses and charged at the stout Brody.

Cole Brody swung around, lifted his Winchester and squeezed its trigger at the riders. Gibson heard the muffled noise of a horse hitting the ground as he began to race across the stable towards the outlaw who was firing his rifle with cold venomous expertise.

Tan Gibson jumped on to the back of Cole Brody and knocked him to the ground. Fists flew in both directions as Gibson smashed the jaw of the large man and then felt his own face being hit by the large knuckles of Brody.

The rifle-butt seemed to come from nowhere and hit the mustang-man on the side of his head. Gibson felt himself falling into a darkness he had not visited for a very long time.

Hitting the ground, Gibson somehow managed to grab on to Brody. He wrestled with the strong outlaw until his eyes cleared again. Then he saw the horses coming straight at them. Hoofs skidded to a halt directly above them and Rainbow and Keno dropped straight on top of the pair.

Yet even the three wranglers could not seem to keep the strong Cole Brody down. He was like a grizzly bear. First he threw Keno off and then Rainbow before staggering to his feet.

Tan Gibson lay on his back and watched helplessly as the raging outlaw lifted his large boot and hovered it above his face.

'Now I'm real angry, mister. You're gonna die. *Adios.*' Brody broke into a slow smile.

Before Gibson could say anything, he saw a hole appear in the centre of Brody's temple. Then a deafening noise echoed all around Pueblo Flats. It was the sound of a single rifle-shot.

Cole Brody staggered backwards and crashed into the large stable door. He seemed to hover for a moment, then blood trickled from the small bullet-hole in the middle of his temple and ran down his swollen face. The ground shook as Brody's body hit it.

Tan Gibson turned around and saw the dust-caked Rufas Blake sitting beside his dead horse, holding on to his smoking Winchester rifle.

'It's the first time I've ever hit anything I was aiming at, Tan,' Rufas said.

'Luckily for me.' Gibson sighed heavily..

Finale

Marshal Vincent and his deputy had somehow managed to survive the perilous journey to the remote Pueblo Flats. They had guided their mounts around the jagged rim of the deep canyons and arrived to find a town covered in the blood not only of citizens but of its attackers.

The morning sun had finally arrived and what it revealed shook the two riders to their very core.

Dismounting beside the stable, the pair of lawmen walked cautiously towards the four exhausted men. Rufas Blake had sewn the deep gash in Tan Gibson's side up tightly with catgut after washing the wound with whiskey. Keno Smith had hogtied the three remaining members of the notorious Brody gang to a fence-pole.

Vincent and Ericson eyed the small

mountain of bodies in the middle of the paddock as they approached the curious Rainbow.

'I'm Marshal Vincent and this is my deputy Ericson.'

Rainbow studied the stars on the men's vests before waving them towards Tan Gibson, who was perched on the edge of a water-trough as Rufas helped him on with his shirt.

'We're on the trail of the Brody gang,' Vincent said to Gibson.

Tan Gibson indicated the dead man lying in the doorway of the livery stable.

'Reckon you found them, Marshal.'

Ericson rushed over to Brody's body and turned it over. Even with a hole in his head, Cole Brody was unmistakable.

'This is Cole Brody, Marshal.'

Vincent stared hard at the body of the man he had hated with such intensity for so many years. He felt cheated.

'There are three of the varmints still alive over yonder and about twenty or so women and children still alive in the bank, Marshal,' Gibson informed Vincent.

Marshal Vincent felt his chin dropping. His long quest for vengeance was at an end. He had not been there at the finish.

'Who are you boys? Are you lawmen?' the marshal asked Gibson as the tall man gathered up the reins to his pinto and slowly mounted it.

Tan Gibson watched as his three tired friends mounted their horses. Rufas Blake had confiscated one of the outlaws' horses to replace the one Cole Brody had shot out from beneath him.

'Nope. We ain't lawmen.'

'You've stopped the most ruthless gang of outlaws in the West and you say you ain't lawmen? Then what are you boys? Bounty hunters? Gunfighters? What?' Vincent watched the four men ease their mounts towards the open gate. As Rainbow, Rufas and Keno cantered out of the paddock, Tan Gibson paused his horse for a moment and looked down at the faces of the two men.

'We're just mustang men, Marshal.'

'Where are you going?' Ericson asked.

'These bastards have a reward on their heads,' Vincent told him.

'We ain't got no time to hang around here, Marshal.'

'Why not?'

'We got us a herd of mustangs to catch.' Tan Gibson tapped his spurs and gently rode at the head of his three friends.

There was a black stallion and at least a thousand wild horses waiting for them..

Soon the paddle steamer would be on its long journey down the Missouri River to St Louis. Now, all Saul Rhymer had to do was to play the last master stroke of the evening. He looked at the mounting pile of gold and dollar bills and again at the cards in his hand. Then, looking around the table, he produced the deed to the goldmine in Montana. 'Let's play poker!' But little did he know how that journey back to St Louis would change his life so drastically.

THE ARIZONA KID

Andrew McBride

When former hired gun Calvin Taylor took the job of sheriff of Oxford County, New Mexico, it was for one reason only — to catch, or kill, the notorious Arizona Kid, and pick up the fifteen hundred dollars reward the governor had secretly offered. Taylor found himself on the trail of the infamous gang known as the Regulators, hunting down a man who'd once been his friend. The pursuit became, in every sense, a journey of death.